"If you crossed the cockeyed wit of Adrian Plass with the hairpin plot twists of Agatha Christie, and threw in a dash of Keystone Kops for flavoring, you'd have something close to Rick Dewhurst's Joe LaFlam and his gumshoe antics. Part slapstick whodunit, part sharp-eyed satire on the contemporary church's fickleness and fetishes, Bye Bye Bertie is as tasty and sticky as a jelly donut, with probably less than half the calories."

Mark Buchanan, Author
Your God Is Too Safe, Things Unseen, and The Holy Wild

"Bye Bye, Bertie by Rick Dewhurst is a quirky, laugh-out-loud tale told by a hapless, juice-fasting gumshoe named Joe LaFlam. Dewhurst's razor-sharp satire exposes many foibles of contemporary churches and worship styles, while his clever prose drives home essential Christian truth. This witty, contemplative, and refreshingly-to-the-point whodunit has enough plot twists and turns to keep readers guessing to the last page. When they get there, readers are likely to shout, 'Way to go, Joe!'"

Ron and Janet Benrey, Authors
Little White Lies, The Second Mile, Humble Pie, and
Dead as a Scone

# BYE BYE BERTIE

## RICK DEWHURST

QUOTIDIAN BOOKS
DUNCAN, BC

Published by Quotidian Books
Duncan BC
Printed in Charleston, SC

ISBN: 0-9867457-1-5
ISBN-13: 978-0-9867457-1-3

*For Jane*

# CHAPTER ONE

I sat, head in my hands, elbows on my desk, praying, oblivious to the peculiar events that were about to unfold around me. There was no mystery of course. Prayer was the answer. So why didn't I do more of it? That was the thorny question. But this Monday morning in November, I was proud of myself. I was really bearing down.

It was 10:30, and I was offering up one of my traditional requests: Would He please send someone, preferably a spiritual giant, to mentor me, so that I would be free to quit my day job and my night job and live a prosperous life of itinerating?

I didn't know what the mentoring process might look like, but I was more than willing to walk it out if itinerating was God's plan for me. On the other hand, if He wanted me to continue in my current profession, I was also more than willing, provided He sweeten the pot with a few lucrative cases. Yes, either way, I had some peace about it.

I was reflecting on the path of self-denial the great ones in the faith had taken—the long years of rejection and mortifying the flesh—when the door of my office opened, and a lovely female head attached to a svelte body in a trim peach suit entered my line of vision.

My heart picked up its pace. She was blonde. Her complexion, pink. Her teeth white, like spotless dice.

"Mr. LaFlam?" she said.

"Joe," I offered.

"Mr. Joe? I must have—"

"No, Joe . . . I'm Mr. Joe LaFlam."

"Oh, Joe."

"Exactly."

I immediately feared the worst. Was our brief misunderstanding prophetic, the sign of a misconceived future together? A life of torment? What would become of our relationship? Were we doomed, and would I never marry? Thirty-three wasn't too old, was it? But perhaps I was getting ahead of myself.

"The detective?"

"In the flesh," I said, offering her a chair, into which she gracefully descended, her right leg crossing over her left and beginning to bounce. She was about twenty-five years old. No wedding band, no engagement ring. Praise God.

Observing me observing her, she said, "I was told you were a Christian."

Oops, busted. I steered my eyes away guiltily. Was my loneliness and deprivation so obvious? Or was the lovely young woman simply overly discerning?

"Uh . . . yes," I said, feeling like a poor witness to my faith.

"Good," she said smiling. "That's why I came to you."

Oh, excellent. She wasn't that discerning after all. I assumed a thoughtful, caring air.

"Problems?" I raised my eyebrows.

"It's my sister."

"Hmm, I see." My brows lowered in understanding.

"She's run away."

"How old?" I said, up with the brows again.

"Her? She's thirty."

"From?"

"Uh . . . from birth?"

"No."

"From what then?"

"Did she run away," I said.

"Yes, that's why I'm here."

"No. From whom did she run away?"

"Oh, I see. Who did she run away from?"

"More or less," I said, now impatient.

"Mummy."

"Oh, dear," I thought and also said.

"Yes, I know," she agreed.

Picking up the scent, I said, "Did she give you or your mother any indication of where she was going?"

"Yes, of course. She left a note. She wouldn't run away without telling us where she was going. After all, she was brought up in a Christian home. But then Daddy died and——"

I cleared my throat.

"Oh, sorry. I'm getting off track . . . the Druids."

"The Druids?"

"Right."

"The ancient Celtic religion?"

"Yes."

"What about it?"

"That's who she's joined."

The light went on.

"You mean, the Druid cult."

Her big, beautiful blue eyes blinked, dropping salty water down her cheeks.

"Bertie's joined a cult," she sniffled through her aquiline nose. The indentation between her nose and upper lip was too short, so that when she talked, the sweet end of her nose bobbed up and down like a rabbit's.

"Bertie?"

"Alberta. Born prematurely on vacation. If they'd had a boy, Dad said, they would have named him Rocky."

I was tossed. She didn't need me; she needed a cult de-programmer, an expert, not a second-rate detective who specialized in finding lost kittens, not a Christian detective who moonlighted part time as a taxi driver to pay the bills. Not that I had a lot of bills as a single man living with my mother.

"I'll take the case. Seventy-five a day plus expenses. And I assure you, I do tithe on that."

She cleared her tears with laced handkerchief dabs and looked grateful, but then, dickering, said, "I don't have much money."

"And Mummy?" I countered.

"Yes, well, OK, we should be able to find it," she said.

"Your name?"

"Oh, sorry, it's Brittany. Brittany Morgan."

"Married?"

"No."

"Boyfriend?"

"No. Not lately."

"Make it fifty dollars a day."

# CHAPTER TWO

I was born in Vancouver, Canada, but later moved to Seattle. And why not? Glued to the American channels as a child, my head had been raised south of the border anyway. I'd always wanted to be an American detective and grow up to fill the gumshoes of my television role models like Mannix and Rockford and Columbo. I admired Americans, and I wanted to be one too. They were more aggressive than those polite Canadians—more entrepreneurial, more litigious. Sure they had their faults, and sure the culture was crumbling, but culture was crumbling all over the Western world. And even though I was coming up short on riches and long on rags, if it was all going down, I wanted to go down American. And even though in Canada the Mounties always got their man, Mounties could never, ever be private detectives. So now I, Joe LaFlam, Christian detective, was much more at home in Seattle than ever I was in that cold, northern Canadian town of Vancouver.

I sat in my office at the corner of Fifth and Marlon, Brittany's morning visit still percolating in the back of my mind. I leafed through *Christianity Today,* wondering how Christians could have so many differing opinions, when the topic of Sunday's sermon sprang from where I had last stuffed it. Snapping to attention, front and center, it shouted, "Fasting, sir!"

Fasting? I wasn't too much interested in the subject. I had survived this long without it. Thirty-three good years. But the pastor was an insistent type—you know, always belaboring pet issues and always at you about something. From among my desk's clutter I grabbed the book I had bought this morning on the subject. Not many in the Christian bookstore written about it, either. That was an indicator of its importance, wasn't it? A lot of nonsense probably.

Imagine giving up food. Not eating for extended periods. Living on water or juice or plain, simple food—anything as long as you didn't like it. A person might die. Would probably get rid of the paunch though.

Still, I was physically fit. Dark brown hair with playful curls. Blue eyes. An even six feet tall. Cute but sturdy. A sturdy, reliable type. That's what I was. And proud of it. I swiveled my chair to face the window, leaned back, and wondered why I had never married.

But there were spiritual benefits to be had from this fasting thing too. That's what our pastor and the book said. Mostly to do with all that spiritual warfare stuff. Stop eating and defeat the adversary, unless, of course, you starved and departed for heaven first. But then you would be a martyr, and the adversary defeated regardless. Win-win situation. And was there food in heaven? What about the Marriage Supper of the Lamb?

I swiveled back to the book.

What was that? Bad breath. The book in front of me, *The Fast Life,* revealed that bad breath was a likely side effect of abstinence from food. No big surprise. An empty tomb for a stomach and all those acids and enzymes with nothing to devour—worse than life on Venus down there, gases bubbling up and out with the potential to sear nose hairs and wither atoms.

Brittany's image beamed into my mind. This wasn't the time for bad breath. No, I couldn't fast now. Besides, I could never tell at the best of times when I had bad breath, even when cupping my hands and forcing hot air out of my mouth and up my nose. Might seem fine and really be foul, and vice versa. So why would I complicate matters with fasting?

And, besides, it was now 2:30—time to go down for a coffee and a jelly donut. I grabbed my black trench coat and blue fedora and headed downstairs, searching my mind for a plan to save Brittany's sister. First, I needed to get the background dope on this crazy Druid cult, and then I needed an overall strategy to deliver Brittany's sister from these brainwashing demons opposed to our American way of life.

Outside the rumbling of mufflers and the splashing of tires in the Seattle rain was replaced by the coffee shop clatter, as the door to the street closed behind me.

"Raining," said Gus the owner. I sat at the counter and he filled my cup.

"Again," I said.

"Another cup?" he said.

"No. The rain."

"Oh," he said, as if he'd just noticed. "Yeah, it's raining again," he said, resigned.

"Raining," Gus repeated, carrying his carafe toward his next victim, a man about my age who had entered after me. He was tall and lean and wore a gray trench coat.

"A jelly donut, will ya, Gus?" I said.

He filled the lean man's cup and then fetched my donut.

"Supposed to stop tonight," Gus said on his way by.

"Hmm," I said, taking a bite and watching the jelly ooze out. Fasting. Who needed it?

Sipping the hot caffeine, I reflected on how God had been reasonably good to me, even though I'd never married. But hold on. I remembered something. I took out *The Fast Life* and found the page, some of the red jelly smearing the edges. There it was. The author, some guy named John Gaunt, said you could get things you wanted by fasting. It was a way of getting His attention; if you were willing to die for it, you might get it. Was that a good method? Twisting God's arm by threatening to starve yourself to death? Who knew? But why not fast for a wife? *The Fast Life* said Daniel fasted for twenty-one days. Yes,

that witnessed to me—a twenty-one-day fast for a wife. No more of
these singles get-togethers at the church. Be specific. That's what you
had to do when fasting and praying. Brittany. Now that was specific.
Twenty-one days of bad breath, and then Brittany and I would tie the
knot.

"Are you Joe LaFlam?" The question came from the tall guy
in the trench coat who had suddenly appeared at my elbow, inter-
rupting my fasting muse.

"In the flesh," I said.

"Brittany sent me."

"Brittany? Where is she? Why didn't she come?"

"Come on," he said. "She asked me to find you."

I gulped what was left of my coffee and shoved in the rest of
the donut.

"On my tab, eh, Gus?" I said, heading for the door.

"Again," Gus said by rote, as the tall man led me back into the
rain.

"Where are we going?" I said, half-running to keep up with his
long, rapid strides.

He neither turned nor answered but led me on. We went about
a block, and then he darted into an alley, a big city alley, the kind
of alley you find in the Pacific Northwest in cities like Seattle, with
cats lurking and stores' backsides fronting either side, their refuse
spilling from garbage bins, oases for the nouveau poor who now
scavenged for discarded, thawing, microwave morsels to eat and
empty bottles to return in exchange for yet another pouch and papers so they could roll more of their death butts.

But why get morbid? The tall man suddenly stopped, turned,
opened a door off the alley, and held it for me until I entered the dark.
I groped around until my eyes adjusted to the light outlining a second
door, which the tall man swung open, revealing about sixty people
facing away from us, in front of their chairs, their hands raised in silence. High on the wall in front of them was a large framed picture of

a blonde girl in a blue uniform who seemed to be the object of their adoration. The door behind me swung closed and nudged me completely into the room.

A picture of Druids at Stonehenge formed in my mind. The tall, lean man walked to an empty chair at the front and, remaining standing, raised his hands high. I found a chair in a back corner, sat down, and hoped Brittany wasn't here. And why the blonde girl in blue? Brittany as a child? A sacrifice? God only knew.

The silence ended with a shriek from the front. I ducked, then peered up to see the head of the one I suspected was the source of the exclamation. She began to pogo-stick, minus the stick. Then bongos began to be beaten and guitar strings began to be strummed. I made a vow (who cared if vows were Old Testament—why quibble?) I would begin my fast at midnight tonight only if Brittany hadn't been eaten. Then the pogoing woman again sounded. "Praise you, Jesus!"

What was that? Jesus? How did He get in here among the idolaters? Then a chorus began. "I'll become even more undignified than this." And then I saw her, Brittany, about halfway up and to the left, clapping to the music. Adrenaline pumped and electricity shot through me; in my stomach, butterfly wings sizzled in acid. The worst had been realized. I had been lured into a church full of charismatics heavily into Renewal. They would be manifesting next. I'd heard all about this kind of thing. Weird stuff. It took a certain kind of Christian to go for all this. But, of course, I was the tolerant kind of Christian, and I certainly wasn't the kind to doubt someone's salvation.

I knew it. Shaking. A few of them up front began to pray for some of the others while the music played on. Jerking too. Yeah, shaking and jerking, and the pogo-sticker was now vibrating like a taut, twanging elastic band. I hated the flesh. No wonder I had never married. Brittany turned and saw me. She smiled ecstatically. My heart leapt. You could get used to this kind of thing. After all, what harm was a little enthusiasm? A gray-haired man in a yellow jumpsuit began to strut around and cluck in a way that could have been interpreted as—that is, if one were to observe with a critical spirit—chicken-like behavior.

Beautiful Brittany glided up the aisle toward me. I waited for my golden angel, as the poultry and the shrieking pogo-sticker faded away.

"I see he found you," she gushed, alive and vibrant. And she was talking to me.

"I'm the one who's supposed to do the finding," I quipped, winking my cute left eye.

"Don't be offended," she said seriously.

"I'm not," I said, wondering why she hadn't picked up on my wink.

"How do you like my church?" she asked expectantly.

"Charismatic?" I offered, dodging her question.

"First Church of the Manifest Presence," she announced proudly.

"Who's the blonde girl in the blue uniform?" I said, pointing to the picture up front.

"Oh, the Girl Guides meet here. We just rent their hall. We don't have our own building. We're a street church."

"Does your sister come here too?"

Suddenly animated and huffy, my sweet Brittany said, "Bertie was too good for us. She and my mother go to a rich Baptist church in the suburbs with the Pharisees . . . all of them Pharisees."

I could see my dear Brittany had manifested one too many times. Something had come loose. That's what usually resulted from all that shaking and jerking and bounding around. And if you didn't do the same, you were automatically a Pharisee. Still, she was likely easier to woo in this condition. And I had lived long enough to know you couldn't have everything.

Suddenly she remembered and sobbed, "At least Bertie used to go to that church until . . ."

My darling sputtered, and then, stomping her pretty, petite feet, blurted, "Before I would have said I would rather she were kidnapped by Druids than to end up a Baptist Pharisee. But now, I don't know."

"I've been thinking about changing churches myself recently," I said, reflecting. "In fact I haven't been attending regularly for the last while. There are some things I just don't agree with where I've been going, and then there's this whole fasting business . . ."

"Oh, do you fast?" she said, now interested, her stomping now stopped, her enthusiasm rising.

"Well . . ."

"It's a fantastic spiritual discipline. Fasting should be mandatory."

"As a matter of fact, I'm just beginning a twenty-one-day fast," I said proudly, at the same time trying to square her hatred of Pharisees with her desire for mandatory fasting. While in pursuit of the elusive mate, I knew, one had to put up with much. Was this why I had never married?

"Partial or absolute?"

"Huh? Oh, a Daniel fast—you eat all the stuff you don't like."

"Cool."

Seemingly satisfied with my upcoming spiritual sacrifice, Brittany fumbled in her pocket and produced a folded piece of paper, which she handed to me surreptitiously.

"Here's why I needed to see you," she whispered.

I read the note as she peered over my shoulder.

"See," she said. "It's a ransom note for $100,000. Bertie's been kidnapped. Can you believe it?"

"I thought she'd run away and joined the Druids."

"She must have changed her mind and then . . ."

"How did you get the note?"

"Mummy found it tucked under Phil's collar."

"His collar? Was that Phil who brought me here?"

"No, Phil's Mummy's pet schnauzer. Bernard would have noticed."

"Bernard?"

"Who brought you . . ."

"That's what I'm asking . . . oh, that was Bernard, the tall guy?"

"He's the associate pastor here."

"He is? Not much of a talker."

Just then, the tall guy, Bernard—the associate pastor, the man who had brought me to this back-lane Renewal church, the First Church of the Manifest Presence, where anything went, it seemed, as far as the expression of worship was concerned—approached and said, "So, Brittany tells me you're a Christian. Are you baptized in the Spirit, brother?"

"How do you mean that?" I said, stalling.

"Do you speak in tongues?"

I was offended. What difference did it make, after all, whether one made those idiotic sounds or not?

"Shushaniah bondai," Brittany said.

"Only in my prayer closet," I said humbly. Man, pursuing the lovely Brittany was becoming increasingly hard on my faith.

"Ah," Bernard said. He nodded and added, "Ahhh."

"Mmm," I rejoined.

"Roogalator hundai," Brittany intoned.

"Hmm," I said.

"It's a heavenly language God gave me," she said. She was obviously proud of it. And who was I to question? I really didn't know what language was spoken in heaven. No, it just wasn't right to judge another in such matters.

"Hmm," I said, nodding. "I see."

"What?" she said.

"Uh, the interpretation," I said.

"You have the gift of interpretation?" Bernard asked.

"Yes, but God just told me not to tell."

"Awesome," Bernard said.

"You'll tell me later?" Brittany said.

I gave her a knowing, confidential look, one I had unearthed from my memory of Tom Cruise in *Mission Impossible*—not that I, a committed Christian, went to movies much. And the ones I did go to usually were related to my private-eye work, like *Mission Impossible,* for instance, or the highly instructive *Naked Gun* series. I needed to go to them for professional development, even though I didn't enjoy them that much, and, of course, I nearly always closed my eyes during the bad bits.

Returning to the job at hand, I studied the ransom note again.

"There's an irregularity here," I said discerningly to Brittany and then looked to Bernard for approval. "They've misspelled Druid. See, it says 'Droid.'"

"So it does," said Brittany, pensive.

"What can it mean?" Bernard added.

"Illiterate?" I offered. Then, pondering, I read the end of the note: "IF YOU DON'T FOLLOW DIRECTIONS TO A TEE, OR IF YOU RAT TO THE POLICE, WE WILL SACRIFICE YOUR LOVED ONE TO ALLAH. SINCERELY, YOUR HEAD DROID."

Bernard said, "Allah's the god of the Muslims."

"He is?" Brittany said, then added, "Imagine sacrificing someone to somebody else's god."

I noted that Brittany's imaginings seemed to lack concern for her sister, but I knew in stressful situations even the most loving of souls might be drawn to the macabre.

She added, "I mean, poor, pure Bertie; don't let them do it to her, Joe. Please, Joe. We have to get them the money."

That was better; more like her. Brittany certainly wasn't the kind to lose her sense of sisterly love, especially at a time like this.

"Poor Bertie. Oh, poor Bertie," she moaned.

My heartstrings tightened for my desolate Brittany. I had to reach out, with the noblest of intentions, to draw her to me, that I might assure her by my embrace that all would be well with her dear sister Bertie. Bernard shot me one of those pastoral "not in the First Church of the Manifest Presence" looks, and my hands fell guiltily before touchdown, but in the same motion my nimble right hand reached into my back pocket and produced a handkerchief to offer my darling to dab her wet eyes. However, she rejected the gesture by looking askance, whereupon I remembered that nobody, not even Christians, used another's handkerchief in these days of exotic bugs.

"I wish I'd been kidnapped instead of Bertie," Brittany said. "Bertie was always the kind one, the smart one." She began to sob again. "And I'm so shallow. Why am I so shallow?"

What could I say? "You're not shallow."

"Yes, yes I am. Mummy knows and Bertie knows. I'm oh, so, so shallow."

"At least you know," I said. Oh, no. "I mean, you can't be that shallow if you know you are. It takes real depth to know you're shallow. So, you see, there's hope."

Stern-faced Associate Pastor Bernard looked at me and then at Brittany. Perhaps sensing there was no hope, he left us and headed for the prayer huddle at the altar below the blonde girl in blue.

"There's hope for Bertie if we deliver the ransom money. Will you do it, Joe?"

"Well, since this case has now become a kidnapping, I'm required to advise you to go to the police."

"Joe, Joe, Joe. You read the note. If we do that, they'll kill her for sure."

"Good enough. Has Mummy raised the money?"

"All she can get is $80,000, Joe, and I don't have any. Hairdressers just don't make that kind of money. What can we do? Poor Bertie."

Until now she had seemed to me to be more like an heiress than an hairdresser. I should have learned to ask questions. There was no way I was going to chip in the extra twenty Gs; that was all

I had, the $20,000 my grandmother had left me. It was going to be the down payment on a house for me and the future Mrs. LaFlam.

"Oh, Joe, what are we going to do? If the Druids sacrifice Bertie to Allah, I'll die. I'll just die. And they've only given us twenty-four hours."

"The church?" I offered lamely.

"We're not a rich church, Joe."

"Your church needs a good teaching on tithing. You can't out-give God, you know."

"Even if we did have the money, we couldn't give the Lord's money to Druids."

"You're right. They sure wouldn't give you a tax-deductible receipt."

"You lost me, Joe," Brittany said softly.

Her eyes sparkled through the tears. Did I see love there? Was it possible? Maybe I would marry after all. But there was no way I was going to give up my inheritance.

"I'll see what I can do," I said.

# CHAPTER THREE

Later that night I sat in my taxi, processing the day's events and waiting for the fasting clock to hit twelve. The night was slow, the way slow nights driving a taxi could be when the rain drizzled down and the dark heart of this Emerald City by the sea beat to the swish-thump of the wiper blades on the windshield of my life.

I had to come up with the money or Bertie was toast, or however they did it. That would spell the end, not only for her but for sweet Brittany and me. But why did it have to be my inheritance? The thought nauseated me, as my stomach began to rumble, and my next thought, the one about going without real food at the stroke of midnight, began to haunt me. No more burgers. What was I to do? A Daniel fast. Who had come up with such a thing? Fruits and vegetables only. Hold on, fries were potatoes and they were a vegetable. No. It was no good; everyone knew fries were a delicacy, and delicacies weren't allowed. Emptiness began to set in. What was my life? Then the image of lovely Brittany again came into focus. Yes, I would do it for her. There was hope. What were twenty-one days out of a life? A mere burp.

"Taxi!" a three-piece suit in an overcoat yelled at me from the curb.

Oh, great, a fare. Just what I needed, more irritation. Just because you drove a cab, people thought they owned you; take me here, take me there. Hold on, what was that? He had a hot dog. I stopped quickly but professionally, as the Small Man tucked his

briefcase under his arm and opened the door, the other hand holding his hot dog.

"Airport," the Small Man said, sliding into the back seat, "and
hurry." The aroma of mustard and onions and fresh-baked bun and
succulent wiener filled the cab. I had to get one before midnight.
Forget the recommended fasting preparation of cleansing your
colon by reducing the garbage intake, I needed a good old American
hot dog in a hurry.

"Good dog?" I said, sniffing and savoring the scent.

"What?"

"Your hot dog smells out of this world."

"You lonely?"

He was being rude. What did he know about a life of sacrifice, a
life of giving with no expectation of reward or recognition?

"No, I'm on a twenty-one-day fast."

"Are you OK to drive?" He seemed concerned.

"No, no, I just started."

"You mean, you're not OK to drive."

"No, I mean I just started the fast . . . well, not quite yet . . . and
the smell of food . . ."

The Small Man became impatient, his voice now edgy, "You
know where the airport is?"

"Sure, don't get excited. I know Seattle like the back of my
hand."

"This is Vancouver."

"Sure, Vancouver, sure. Relax, I know the way to the airport."

I was going to tell him I was foodless in Seattle, but why annoy
him further? He popped in the last of his dog and sat back, lost in
his life.

"I'm foodless in Seattle," I said, forgiving him his rudeness.

"Would you just drive?"

The Small Man was small and in his midfifties with black or
maybe brown hair and a blue suit; it was hard to identify the colors

accurately in the dark, as I snatched glimpses in the rearview mirror, the lights of oncoming cars flashing in my eyes. He had a tan overcoat and round, wire-framed glasses. But what did his appearance matter? He was just another fare to me——the kind of fare you picked up in the big city where anonymity reigned, where the rugged individual was king as long as you had the money to pay the fare. Yes, this was the big city where nobody cared whether you were a businessman or whether you worked for the government or whether you were a banker or a baker or a hockey-stick maker. In this, our republic, it was all the same when you wanted to get from A to B. This was America, where all you needed was enough dough-ray-me to pay the price of the fare and enough courage to go for the ride.

"Which terminal?" I said casually.

"Departures."

"Domestic or international?"

"International."

"Leaving the country, eh?"

"OK, if it'll make your day, I'm flying to Washington."

"Then you want domestic flights?"

Teeth gritted, he said, "Take me to the international departure terminal."

"OK, you're the boss," I said. He was obviously a small man in the grand scheme of things.

When I dropped him off at the terminal, I briefly weighed whether I should go in for an expensive, airport hot dog or make the five-minute trip to the 7-Eleven, where I could throw my own together at a fraction of the cost. To practice exercising my willpower for the days of deprivation ahead, I bravely chose the second option.

Racing to my rendezvous with fast food, I massaged my hurt feelings. He hadn't even given me a tip. Yes, the rich got richer and the poor got poorer. That's the way it was in America, whether you lived back in the days of Al Capone or Richard Nixon, or whether you lived now, in the dark nights of the post-industrial, cyberspace, virtual-reality cosmos; the dollar was the deal.

At the 7-Eleven I loaded my ninety-nine-cent delicacy with all the trimmings and returned to my cab, where I noticed that the Small Man had forgotten his briefcase in the backseat. In his elitist rush to pay his fare and to remove himself from the presence of one whom he no doubt perceived to be the working poor, he had become careless. I stood and looked at it while I finished the last bite. Then I ran back into the store and bought a giant bag of potato chips and a large cola slurpee.

When I returned, the briefcase was still lying there on the backseat, a seat where over the years nearly every possible . . . but there was no profit in carrying on thinking in that direction. I got into the driver's seat and reached back for the briefcase, but before looking into it for ID, I opened the potato chip bag and munched a few, remembering that in America chips were only potato chips, whereas in Canada you could call french fries "chips" and everyone knew what you were talking about. But in America if you asked for chips, you would never get french fries, and you just had to get used to the idea.

I chomped a few more handfuls and then remembered something else. The faint, distant image in my rearview mirror, as I sped away to get my hot dog, of the Small Man stepping into the street and waving his arms.

I ran my fingers over the expensive, fine-grained, black leather briefcase, leaving a trail of cheap grease. There was no sense in stalling. I popped it open, surprised it wasn't locked. Inside was a single document, held together with a paper clip. The cover page read, "DISSOLVING BORDERS: Toward the Unification of the Americas." *Catchy title.* I flipped to page 2. The study had been written by committee and proposed the unification of the Americas into one political entity, which would better facilitate, it said, the establishment of a one-world government. The plan had been commissioned by some group called the Gardenbergers, a group I remembered hearing about in association with environmental and animal rights issues. It also said the Gardenbergers were connected to something called Spelunkers Global.

If I had my conspiracy theory facts right, the Grand Royal Order of the Spelunkers Global was a secret society that was clandestinely erecting mini-pyramids in the sewer systems of every major city in the world for the insidious purpose of creating an underground power matrix that would bind the planet together for all time, and once in place would initiate the beginning of the Age of the Dirty Rat. None of this could be proved, however, especially since there were many, many miles of underground sewers in the world, and nobody in the know had yet volunteered to check them all out.

The scary part of this document was the list of names endorsing its contents. I could see there was a lot of money behind this scheme. Most conspiracy theorists on the Internet insisted there were insidious forces at work with plans to take over the world. But the question always was, Who actually were these conspirators? Who was in and who was out? The answer was here. The names on this list were all high-ranking government and business leaders from the most powerful countries in the world, including the American president, the Canadian prime minister, and the secretary general of the United Nations. Several pages described how they were all linked with their counterparts in other countries through this elite organization, Spelunkers Global.

The truth at last. They had been working underground for years all over, or under, the planet, no doubt erecting mini-pyramids everywhere they descended, leaving bad vibrations in their subterranean trail.

But what was their purpose? What were they trying to do? What I found on the last two pages stunned me. Their plan was truly beyond human imagination, even beyond the twisted rambling of most conspiracy theorists.

"Put the papers slowly into the briefcase and close it."

The cab door had opened suddenly behind me and a hard, pointed object pressed into my neck. The voice was coming from the backseat from the vocal chords of the Small Man. I recognized its tinny quality. It was the same voice that had said, when he'd gotten out of the cab at the airport, "I'll give you a tip, all right. If you don't eat, you'll die."

"Now hand it back over to me . . . that's good. Now start the car. Put the chips down . . . say, I thought you were . . . oh, never mind . . . and you got grease on my briefcase. You're going to pay for that. Pull out and go north on Highway 1."

"You mean I-5."

"Sure, why not? You don't have much longer to play your head games."

I knew now I was done for; my life's short journey was coming to a close. I drove, I just drove, reflecting on the long years of childhood, the glory days when the ozone was thicker and the sun wouldn't kill you so fast, when you could still play in the sunshine without thought of tomorrow, when innocence was. . . .

"Turn off here."

And then came the teen years and graduation and going to the prom with Becky, the only girl to say yes.

"OK, pull over."

I doubted I would have time to remember my twenties and then wondered why my life hadn't passed before my eyes a lot faster, and then I was sorry my highlights were pretty lame, and then I truly wondered why I had never married, and then I suspected I truly never would.

"Get out."

I got out of the car with the Small Man still at my back. We were on a back country road, no houses around, no streetlights.

"You're a Small Man," I said bravely.

"Taller than you," he said tersely.

"Sure, you're big for a mole."

"You shouldn't have stuck your nose in."

"Is it midnight yet?" I asked.

"Past."

"No more chips, then. I've had my last meal."

"You've got that right. Get moving into those trees."

"Why are you doing this?" I said, making my way through the underbrush.

"My father never affirmed me and my mother drank."

"No, I mean, why are you going to kill me? Just because I know about some ridiculous underground conspiracy to take over the world?"

"You don't think that's enough?"

"You mean, it's true? All those world leaders and bankers and corporation heads are . . . are Spelunkers?"

"Exactly. And now you know too much. Say your prayers."

"Oh, Lord . . . well, here I am for the last time. Please forgive me for never making much of myself, for wasting my life, really, but I guess that doesn't mean anything now, when it comes right down to it."

"Oh, shut up."

The image of Brittany flashed in my mind. She was dancing at her church beneath the Girl Guide, she and the pogo-sticker, the senior chicken, and Bernard—a wistful sight—and then I wondered if I were dead and just hadn't heard the gun go off. No, I was still alive; I could hear the Small Man wheezing behind me. I turned as he staggered and braced himself against a tree.

"Stop or I'll shoot," he sputtered.

"I'm not going anywhere," I said innocently.

He dropped his gun, clutched his chest, and fell to the forest floor with a muffled, rustling thud. "Heart . . ." he choked, "Get . . . hospital."

I was confused. Had the benefits of fasting paid off already, even though it was barely past midnight? Had fasting saved me? Or had I been saved by a hot dog. His bad baby-boomer eating habits had, no doubt, contributed to high cholesterol levels, culminating in his current condition, his recent hot dog having squeezed in the last wedge to halt the works.

Now the question was, had I been saved by the spiritual effects of fasting or the carnal causality of bad diet? Or had they somehow worked together—the flesh and the spirit? It was no small question either because why would I carry on fasting if the flesh could save me? Besides, I still had lots of potato chips in my cab, and maybe that was a sign.

"Please," he whimpered.

I opted to defer my decision. I picked up and pocketed his gun. I then threw the Small Man over my shoulder and carried him to the cab. I opened the door and gently dropped him on the backseat.

Getting into the driver's seat and picking up the mike, I realized there was a good chance I would marry after all.

"Car sixty-six," I said.

"Go."

"I've got a sick baby boomer on board . . . headed for emergency ward."

"Ten-four, sixty-six."

"The baby boomers took everything. They lived off the fat of the land and in the process clogged their arteries. They weren't content with enough; they wanted more and more. And now the planet is plundered, and guess who'll have to foot the bill for them?"

"Get off the radio, sixty-six."

"Hurry," moaned the boomer in the back.

# CHAPTER FOUR

The next morning I sat depressed at the kitchen table. The thought of twenty-one days of eating vegetation was gnawing on my brain. There had to be another way. Yes, what about substitutes? What about veggie burgers, for instance? They were just ground-up beans glued together somehow, and beans were a vegetable. Yes, you had to give them credit; vegetarians were slick when it came to aping beef.

But no, there was probably something dishonest about eating food that looked like food that wasn't allowed on your fast. Eating meat impersonators was deceitful. And Daniel probably never had the luxury of bean burgers, so why should I?

And, besides, I had other things on my plate to think about: the Small, Nearly Dead Man, for instance, and what to do with his briefcase and gun, and then there was Brittany and her sister and the Druids and the ransom money. What about the police, who just might have a few questions if they knew the situation, because kidnapping was still a dirty word in this town, and what about my inheritance and the rent due on my office and a 101 other things that afflicted you in this busy, city life in the new millennium in the United States of America, soon to become one with the rest of the continent if the Spelunkers Global had their way? And it looked like they just might, given their rich and powerful membership, and . . . .

"If you took divorce cases, you wouldn't always be short of money," my mother said sternly from across the kitchen table. "And then you wouldn't have to drive a taxi all night to pay the rent on that office, though I don't know what you need an office for anyway; all you do is sit in it."

Mother punctuated her financial advice by snapping off a quadrant of toast with her new teeth. It was obvious she hadn't buttered her toast while it was hot from the toaster, but rather had let it cool, until it was hard, and then she had buttered it. But, of course, the butter hadn't melted. How could butter melt at that temperature?

"Why are you staring at my toast?" Mother said between crunches.

My upper lip began to moisten. My insides were cold.

I said, "If you butter it right away, when it's hot out of the toaster, the butter will melt and the toast will soften, and then it won't crunch and scatter crumbs everywhere."

"Are you getting enough sleep, dear? And why aren't you eating your Cheerios this morning?" Her face suddenly gleamed. "Could it be . . . have you found someone?"

"Yes," I said.

"Why then . . . ?"

"It's complicated."

"Oh, I see. Never mind, dear. It always is. Eat. You'll need your strength."

"I . . . I won't be eating regular food."

"Oh, no. She's not a vegetarian . . . oh, my poor boy."

"No, Mother, she's not. I'm fasting for awhile, that's all."

"Oh. I see. How long?"

"Twenty-one days."

"You'll be needing something for your breath then."

"I know."

Mother snapped another shard of toast, fragments flying everywhere. Despite her slipping eating habits, Mother was still what would be called attractive. Her long brown hair, parted in the middle, gave her a dried-flower-child quality, fragile and delicately preserved. She passed a lot of her time creating arts and crafts in her workshop above the garage.

"What's her name?" she said.

"Brittany."

"Classy."

"What's she do?"

"She's an hairdresser."

"Hmm. There'll always be a room for you here, dear."

My mother lifted her tea, slurped, and "hmmed" again. Her "hmms" didn't bother me today. But my ardor for Brittany had cooled just the same, exactly as *The Fast Life* had predicted it would.

Apparently, fasting killed the sex drive. Food was more crucial than procreation on the list of essential things needed to sustain life. If you didn't have food, then who cared about doing anything else. You could drop dead any minute, and then what good would a wife be? I had to examine just how much of my attraction to Brittany was simply on a physical level. And if that's all there was, I might as well keep on fasting, and at the moment I wasn't sure I cared if I ever married.

My mother pretended not to burp and said, "Is that her real name?"

I needed help. There was too much going on in my life right now, and no one to tell it to. I needed to talk it all out, like they did on *Friends,* only in a Christian context, but then again Christians wouldn't be all living together like that. I hated *Friends.* But at least I had homegroup tonight. I could talk there.

I gulped my orange juice and wondered if Day 1 would ever end, and it was now only 8:00 A.M. I remembered the commandment to honor your parents and said, "Yes, as far as I know, that's her real name."

"You don't seem happy about it."

"I'm happy. Only I've got to get to the bank when it opens. I've got a deadline."

"Don't worry, dear. Time will pass."

# CHAPTER FIVE

I sat in my office with my twenty grand in small bills on the desk in front of me. I felt empty. Brittany, money. Money, Brittany. Oh, well, what was money? You couldn't eat it. I had to readjust my thinking, that was all. This fasting state was the unnatural one. My current lack of passion for Brittany was temporary. Deprivation had altered my brain chemicals. Starved synapses were misfiring, no doubt rendered impotent by the absence of good beef protein. Once the fast was over, I would be back to normal. And besides, wasn't it the Christian thing to do? Help a distressed, Christian sister in her time of need when no one else was there to care for her?

And not only that, my sister's sister was also in need, and of course she, also, was my Christian sister, whether she had a Pharisaical bent or not. Dear Bertie in the earthy hands of Druids. Her fate was sealed without my intervention. Yes, Grandmother would have understood my risking my inheritance. Grandmother wouldn't have risked it, of course, but she would have understood my doing it.

A soft knock came and Brittany entered, carrying a valise. She was wearing that same peach suit, and her hose weren't quite straight, a tuft of nylon escaping the heel of her purple left shoe, which was scuffed on the toe to match the other one. She sat down, anxious.

"Oh, Joe," she said, eyeing the cash, "you came up with the money."

I spun in my chair and halfway around gave my mouth a quick blast of breath freshener. Facing her, I immediately saw something I hadn't noticed before; her left eyelid drooped slightly lower than the right one, and her eyes themselves were milky in the blue part. And somehow her shape had lost its appeal.

Impatient and petulant, I said, "Here, twenty thousand . . . where's the other eighty?"

She hoisted her valise to the desk and opened it. Inside were stacks of bills.

"Fine," I said, resigned, and shoveled my contribution into it.

She closed the clasp with a click. But I wasn't going to let my inheritance go that easy. I had a plan.

"I've got a plan," I said.

Brittany came around to my side of the desk, sat on the edge facing me, and leaning in, said, "I'm all ears."

I wondered if she had been fasting too. I fingered the spearmint aerosol in my pocket and then thought better of it.

I said, "Let's review the drop-off instructions."

She laid the ransom note on the desk and twisted slightly to read it with me.

"OK." I said. "I take the money to the park. I get off at the zoo and stuff the valise in the garbage can in front of the monkey cage and then leave without looking back."

"That's it, Joe. It's all set for noon. It's simple. That's all you have to do. And Bertie will be free. My darling sister will be free." She reached over and rested her skinny fingers on my shoulder. "We're free too, Joe," she said. My mind, interpreting freedom preferentially, flashed on an image of the Golden Arches.

"Let's be realistic for a minute here. We don't know if they will release your sister or even if . . . if she's still alive. Sorry, I had to say it. We both know that kidnappers seldom release their victims."

"We do?" she said.

"Yeah, never mind . . . I've got a plan," I repeated.

"Oh, you're so smart, Joe. What's your plan?"

"I'm going to stash a disguise in the men's restroom on the edge of the park, and then instead of leaving, I'm going to change quickly—two, three minutes tops—and then double back and stake out the garbage can."

"Sounds dangerous, Joe, especially for Bertie. Are you sure you can be quick enough and they won't recognize you?"

"Positive. And I'll have my '75 Mustang parked nearby in case I have to tail whoever picks up the money. They're not getting my inheritance that easy."

"But what about Bertie?"

"If she's still alive, they'll lead me right back to her, and maybe, just maybe, they'll have already let her go. In which case I'll liberate our money."

"It'll be dangerous, Joe."

"No problem. I'm packing my .22-automatic."

"Well, Joe?"

"Yeah, it's showtime. Let's go. But first I've got to pay a visit to the washroom down the hall."

# CHAPTER SIX

I don't know exactly when or how she switched valises," I summarized to my church homegroup that night. "But it really doesn't matter somehow."

There were only five others at homegroup, including the leaders, Mavis and Don. They had been listening to my story for about ten minutes now in their spacious living room, and, for the most part, they had been Christian about it, except maybe for Abner, who had shaken his head a few times in a way that could have been interpreted as condemning.

"It's not your fault. There was clearly no scriptural precedent for such a situation," said Lily, the group's self-appointed theologian.

"Clear case of lust," Abner said. "And ya reaped yer just reward."

Abner had only recently been saved from a life of alcohol and drug abuse, so I had to appreciate his candor.

Lily's husband, Ben, said, "Have a little mercy, Abner. You were young once."

"But I haven't wanted to be no private eye since I was twelve." Abner shook his head again and then chuckled, "Private eye, my eye. I can just see him rootin' around in the garbage can in the dark in his Sherlock Holmes outfit. Who'd ya think ya were foolin'—the cage of monkeys?"

Abner wheezed out his laughter, shaking his sandy-gray hair. His stubbled face with its red-leather complexion, weathered from years of abuse, was now nearly purple.

"OK," Don said. "We need to—"

"I hate to take up so much time," I interrupted, "but there's something else. Yesterday I stumbled across a conspiracy to take over the whole planet."

"You the only one who gets to talk here?" Abner asked. "I've gotta few things about my life I'd like to share . . . like what am I goin' to do about chewin' after leavin' my lower plate in Denny's, and it hasn't turned up yet. How's that for a global conspiracy. And who knows? Maybe it was those Druids who stole my choppers, using them to——"

Just then Lily spoke up. "How did you find out about this conspiracy, Joe?"

"One of my fares left a briefcase in my cab. When I looked inside for ID, I found the papers."

"Snooper," Abner said. "That's all you private eyes is, is snoopers. A cab-driving private eye. What a picture . . . I'd run and tell the grandchildren if I knew I had any."

"We'll pray for you later, Abner," Don said. "But now let's hear what Joe's got to say. He's had a rough day."

"And I suppose a rough life don't count right now," Abner said.

Don gave Abner a firm look, to which Abner said, "Sure, OK. I'll shut up."

"Carry on, Joe," Mavis said.

"I'll come to the point for Abner's sake," I said. "The Small Man came back for his briefcase and was going to kill me for what I'd found out. But he had a heart attack before he could pull the trigger. He's in the hospital now."

"We should make a note of that," Lily interjected, "his name, hospital, etc., so that the church pastoral care and visitation team can . . ."

Mavis wilted Lily with a look.

"Here's the scoop," I said. "Leading politicians and business people from nearly every country on earth are plotting to take over the planet to form a one-world government."

"But that's old news," Ben said. "We all know that. What's so hush-hush that he was going to kill you?"

"Spelunkers."

"Spelunkers?" Ben said, echoed by Mavis and Don.

"You mean, cave explorers?" Mavis said.

"That's right," I said. "They're set to take over the world."

"And just how are they going to do that?" Mavis inquired.

"I told you . . . waste of time," Abner mumbled.

"Remember that Lord Maitraya guy we heard about a few years ago, and then lately we've heard nothing about him? Well, it seems he went underground, and the plan now is that pretty soon Mother Earth, or 'Gaia' they call her now, is going to give birth to Maitraya. Then he'll emerge from his earth womb a sort of Gaia Maitraya. But first they're going to cause chaos for us here on the surface. A nuclear weapon here, a deadly virus there—that kind of thing. And while all that's going on, the business and the government leaders, who are secret members of Spelunkers Global, will disappear underground to join Maitraya, and that will cause even more chaos with nobody left here in charge. And everyone will be wondering where all the leaders went."

Abner mumbled, "He should've killed ya."

"But that's not the worst part. The plan is that once underground, they'll all enter these prefab cocoons they've got stashed everywhere—they'll be in them for three weeks or so—where they'll undergo a biotech metamorphosis. And this is the killer: they then emerge from their cocoons transformed into a bunch of Bill Clintons."

"Holy Dinah, all hail Bubba!" Abner shouted.

"And then comes the rupture. They surface all over the world to bring order out of chaos, with Maitraya as the head Clinton, a foot taller and fifty pounds heavier than the others. That's the plan; Gaia Maitraya in larger-than-life Clinton form, sitting enthroned, the Lord of the Earth."

"Diabolical," Lily said.

"I've got proof. I've got the guy's gun and the papers in his briefcase in my safe at the office. I didn't want to bring them here and put you at risk."

Abner said, "But you just told us——"

"Never mind," Don said. "We have nothing to fear; we know how this all ends. We've read the end of the Book." Don waved his Bible.

"I haven't got that far yet," Abner said. "How does——?"

"We're living in exciting times," Mavis said.

# CHAPTER SEVEN

I woke up on my office couch the next morning, aching and depressed. The room through my gritty eyes was unsteady. My head was splitting, and my eyelids were burning. I sat up, and my stomach began to thump like it was going to heave nothing but bitter yellow bile. My tongue lay heavy under its rough coat.

I slowly stood and gently moved to the mirror. Looking in wasn't pretty. Then I remembered what I had said last night at homegroup. And then I remembered and regretted what I had done later. Abner was right. I would have been better off now if the Small Man had killed me. I'd made a big mistake this time. The impact of losing my inheritance and discovering the truth about Brittany had propelled me off the deep end.

When I left homegroup, I was so desperate and lonely I did something I now wished had never entered my mind. But there was no point in making excuses. I had to be a man about it. The Lord would hold me accountable. But now, this morning, I wondered what I had been thinking.

How could I have, even though I had been in great distress, abandoned the Daniel fast and vowed to the Lord to live on only juice for the next twenty days? Yes, the pain was bad, but that's what *The Fast Life* said would happen as the toxins began to break down and be expelled from your system. On the positive side, the dinner-gong, caffeine-deprivation headache was bound to keep me focused.

The idea had seemed sound last night. I would bear down on this fast, and God would change His mind about me. My life would turn around. I would prosper with His direct help. He would inter-vene and find me a wife—the perfect one for me. And perhaps He would call us into full-time ministry, so I would not have to work anymore, and we would be happy, self-sacrificing missionaries to the hurting people of the world. That was last night, but today I saw nothing but pain.

As I journeyed over to my desk, a firm knock hit my door, which opened, and a female head appeared with eyes that sternly stared at me. The head came farther in, and with it came its body.

"Joe LaFlam?" the head said from its mouth.

I was in no mood to answer, even though, when I perused her whole package, she seemed worth answering.

"Are you sick?" the person asked.

Oh, all right, I'll answer. "Yes and yes."

"Well, I am happy you are Joe LaFlam, and I am sorry you're sick."

"Fair enough," I thought and said.

"I'm Bertie Mulligan. May I?"

"Sure, sit down. Hmm. That's odd."

"What is?"

"You're a Bertie, and I never knew a Bertie, but I knew a Bertie's sister, and now you're a Bertie too."

"Are you OK? Perhaps I . . ."

"No, I'm fine, well, I am sort of." Momentarily light in the head, I took my chair for a spin and halfway around shot a squirt in.

Returning, I said, "But her Bertie was a Morgan, not a Mulligan, and so was she."

"My sister's name is Brittany."

"You don't say," I said, feeling giddy. Maybe starvation would be good for me and fun. My empty stomach let out an extended growl.

"Speaking in Tums," I said glibly to her raised eyebrows.

She smiled. "Our church believes the gifts died out with the apostles."

"And what do you believe, young lady?"

She frowned. "Young lady? Well, I certainly don't believe in unilateral female submission to male authority, and I happen to be thirty years old."

"Ever marry?"

"Not yet."

"Hmm."

She wasn't plain; she was more attractive than that. The brown hair wasn't mousy; it was tidy and went well with her overall sharpness. Her figure was all there and trim, but I had difficulty discerning in my fasting state what my normal response might be to her total appearance.

She said, "You look like you're judging horseflesh."

"Oh, sorry. I'm a little disoriented. You see, I'm kind of . . . you know . . . fasting. Not that simple Daniel kind either. No, I'm on the straight juice kind, and only clear fluids too—no pulp or anything like that mixed in to keep the bowel moving. No, my bowel will be completely shut down for the duration. Yeah, for the next twenty days I'll be living on liquid."

"How spiritual of you and needlessly candid. But since you're in a mood for disclosure, how long have you been fasting now?"

"Well, it's a twenty-one-day fast in total."

"So, you've been fasting one day."

"Well, to be accurate, this is the second day."

I discerned this was no ordinary woman, but then again there probably were no ordinary women. Being a detective, I knew I should learn to ask questions. But was I really that anxious to know? OK, fine, why not? The subject did need changing.

"Have you got a picture of your sister?" I asked.

"Why? Are you taking the case?"

"What case?"

"Getting my sister back."

"She's missing? No, don't tell me. She's been kidnapped."

"Yes. That's why I came to you. She's been kidnapped by Druids."

"You came to the wrong place, sister. I'm already broke. And you're not getting my car."

"I was planning to pay you."

"So, of all the private detectives in all of the offices in all of the buildings in all of this big town of Seattle, how is it you walked into mine?"

"I found your card among my sister's things. And as far as I know, this is Vancouver."

"Sure, whatever." I knew trouble now. In my short time on this crazy planet I'd already encountered enough in the last few days to last me a lifetime. So she was the "sister Bertie" of Brittany's scam. Sisters in crime.

"You're a Christian?" I asked.

"Yes, of course," she answered.

Christian sisters in crime. Blood sisters and brethren sisters too.

"How stupid do you think I am?" I wanted to know.

"Well," she said, pondering, "I haven't known you long enough to give you an informed response to your question, but judging by our conversation so far, I would say you are borderline incompetent. How that might relate to your intelligence, or as you put it, your stupidity, could best be assessed by my asking if, perhaps, you have had adequate training and experience to be practicing your profession, or if you have been under too much stress or strain lately. . . ."

"OK, OK. You win. I'm no James Bond. But I'm smart enough to know when I'm being played for a sucker. Nobody's going to make a monkey out of me twice."

"Do you want this job or not?" she said, now impatient.

"Relax. First let me see if I understand the job. You want me to take the ransom money and stuff it into the garbage can in front of the monkey cage in the park."

"That's amazing. I retract my initial assessment of your competence. How did you know that?"

"Experience. Now, let's get to the hitch."

"Hitch?"

"Yeah, you know—the part about not having enough ransom money."

"I've got enough. We have the ransom money."

"You do? Who's we?"

"My mother and I."

"And I suppose you're rich?" I was getting good at asking questions, and I was beginning to enjoy asking them too.

"Well, by most standards we are. My father, when he died, left us controlling interest in his national hotel chain."

"So why does Brittany have to work as an hairdresser?"

"Hairdresser? She never worked a day in her life."

"So she is an heiress and not an hairdresser."

"Yes. That's, of course, why they've targeted her. Do you know a Brittany who's an hair . . . I mean, a hairdresser?"

I ignored her question. "You've probably got lots of influence in this town; why haven't you gone to the police? In fact, it's my duty right now to advise you to go to the police."

"We can't," she said, tears beginning to form. "Read this."

She handed me a note and pointed to the now-familiar content: "IF YOU DON'T FOLLOW DIRECTIONS TO A TEE, OR IF YOU RAT TO THE POLICE, WE WILL SACRIFICE YOUR LOVED ONE, BRITTANY MULLIGAN, TO THE DRUID GOD. SINCERELY, YOUR HEAD DRUID."

At least Brittany had done her editing or found somebody to do it for her.

"OK," I said, "what's the game?"

"Clearly you can see it's not a game. They're going to kill my sister if we don't give them $200,000 by noon tomorrow."

"What do you mean 'we'? And why only $200,000? Why not two million?"

"I don't know. I don't know how the Druid mind works."

"There are no Druids. Brittany's mind is the mind. Do you know how hers works?"

"What are you saying? If we don't give them the money, they're going to kill her."

"Stop saying 'we.'"

"I came here for help not ridicule. I thought you might be trustworthy since Brittany had your business card. Don't you private investigators have some kind of ethical code? And your card also says you're a Christian detective. Don't you have any compassion?"

Good question. My compassion had nearly left me last night, when I finally smelled a double cross, and rifling through the trash can in the dark, in the rain, the tobacco in my Sherlock pipe damp, I discovered the switched valise full of ripe bananas. There I was, my inheritance gone, staring at the monkey cage and sucking wet tobacco. Then the police cruiser pulled up and took me in for questioning. That's when my compassion left me completely. I was almost late for homegroup.

"No," I said.

"Well, I suppose that's all there is to be said." She gave her tears a wipe, and her nose a blow and a swipe, as she rose from her chair. There was something compelling about her. I was strangely drawn to her. Perhaps it was the way she wielded her dainty handkerchief, or maybe it was the sound of her life's breath rushing out from her nostrils; whatever, I only knew I had to keep her there, keep her there with me, if only to explore the depths of my own despair.

"OK, relax. Sit down. I don't turn people away just because I suspect they're trying to con me into something."

She looked at me quizzically. "What? You should turn people away if that's what they're trying to do," she said.

"Not me," I said. "I don't want to be perceived as intolerant."

"You should be intolerant of dishonesty," she said, resuming her seat.

"I want to be a good witness . . . you know, turn the other cheek. Anyway, just about everybody out there is trying to con you into something or other. You'd end up not talking to anybody. So I try to be a good witness—a tolerant Christian—especially with my clients. Take your sister for instance. She came in here claiming you had been kidnapped by Druids."

"What? Me? What are you saying? She's the one who—"

"No. She came in here a few days ago, claiming her sister Bertie had been kidnapped, and she wanted me to deliver the ransom money, and, by the way, she was short a few thousand, twenty thousand to be exact, and asked if I could make up the difference, and I did, and now she's gone, and my inheritance is gone, and now I can't eat food, only drink juice, and then you, sister Bertie, come in here expecting me to believe Brittany's been kidnapped by Druids, and ask if I would deliver the ransom money, which you say you have in full, but I know there's a catch, a catch where I end up worse off than I was, probably without a car, and an office, and my mother throws me out of the house, and I'm living on the street, sleeping under cardboard, or maybe just newspapers, and I haven't eaten food in days because I'm fasting, and I'll never, ever marry because who in her right mind would want to come and share my cardboard in some alley where only the rats have worse breath than I."

"Please. You're becoming hysterical. Calm down. Where's your faith?"

"What do you mean, my faith? I'm willing to do all that to be a good witness, and you say I don't have any faith."

I began to sob. I had lost everything, and I knew that only God would have me now.

"Maybe you should eat something," she said. "I think lack of food has altered your brain chemistry."

"I can't. I made a vow," I said, attempting to regain my dignity. "And besides, it's only the poison coming out of my system. *The Fast Life* tells all about it. I'll recover."

My brief outburst had subsided, and now I felt stronger for the release and more at peace.

"OK," I said. "If you're not in this with Brittany; if you're legit and you really do have the ransom money, then you would be throwing it away. Brittany's behind all this. She took me for twenty grand, and now she wants your two hundred Gs."

"I've tried my best so far not to comment, but please stop your periodic injection of that 1940s detective slang; under the stress of my circumstances it's becoming unbearable."

"Sorry. By the way, while we're on the subject, where did you learn your lingo, from one of those exclusive women's colleges?"

"Yes, as a matter of fact, I did. Are you satisfied?"

"Yeah, I'm satisfied. I know I shouldn't be satisfied, not by any upper-middle-class, North American standards at least, but I am generally satisfied, except perhaps for my low income and the fact that I'm not married and I'm living with my mother, and there's not much hope I'll ever make the big time in my chosen profession, and I'm secretly ridiculed by other Christians because I'm different, but I'm not bitter; I still have hope . . . hope that Jesus, by His grace, turns my life around, and if not, then He at least comes back real soon and rescues me from all this."

"What is the matter with you?"

"I told you. It's the toxins."

"I do sympathize, but don't you understand? My sister is in great danger. They're going to kill her if we don't deliver the ransom money by noon tomorrow."

"There you go with 'we' again. So, all right. Let's just say she was kidnapped. Who's to say they haven't killed her already? You know as well as I do that kidnap victims aren't usually released alive."

"Of course she was kidnapped. She's missing, and I showed you the note. What more do you need? And she has to be alive. I won't have it any other way."

Why me? There really had to be something wrong here. I definitely smelled a rat. Not that I really knew what a live rat smelled like because I had never been right up close to a real live one. But I knew what a dead rat smelled like when it died in the walls, after nibbling the blood-thinning poison you'd left for it and you couldn't get it out without tearing the Sheetrock down, not that you'd have wanted to find it, smelling like that, so you just had to wait a week or two until the aroma died down and you really hoped that the next one wouldn't die in the walls in the kitchen.

"Excuse me," I said, gagging and running for it. Inside my bathroom I observed, wide-eyed, my Dizzy Gillespie cheeks in the mirror as I bravely forced the heaves back down. I knew I had to hold myself together. I didn't want to give fasting a bad name. I asked God to help me, while I did some deep breathing. Satisfied my stomach was settled, I exited the washroom, resolved to discover from Bertie's story what smelled so fishy, or at least find out what was rotten in Denmark. I turned, reentered the washroom, snubbed Dizzy in the mirror, and went straight for the bowl. I knelt until my knees hurt.

"Are you all right?" the concerned voice said from the other side of the door.

"I've got a question for you," I said, gasping. "Why don't you deliver the money yourself? Why do you need me?"

"My mother advises strongly against that," she said through the door. "Brittany has already been kidnapped, and she doesn't want me in any danger."

"Why come to me? You could hire the best."

"Your card says you are a Christian detective, and as I said before, I found your card among Brittany's things, so I thought you were the . . . I mean . . . well, this is ridiculous, I know, but now for some strange reason I kind of . . . like you."

I felt one eyebrow raise and then my head. I mopped my mouth with tissue from the roll.

"Hello," she called. "Are you . . . ?"

"Yes, I'm fine, I'm coming. Nothing to be concerned about . . . a trivial fasting hazard is all, to be expected on the more advanced, clear-fluid fast. Part of the discipline. Be right with you."

I was well enough now to imagine what Bertie truly might look like if I were eating. Yes, definitely. More than adequate. I might marry after all, and I had a plan. It was obvious now that Brittany had used me as a warm-up for the big score. A little extra spending money before she hit the big time. The only thing she hadn't counted on was that Bertie would find my card and come to me. But why would darling Brittany go through all this to get money that she would eventually get anyway? I wouldn't be satisfied until I uncovered the answer to that one.

Meanwhile, my destiny awaited on the other side of the door. Would Bertie be mine? Was that part of the overall plan? I gave my mouth a triple squirt, satisfied that Bertie wasn't in cahoots with her sister, and then opened the door to the rest of my life.

Bertie had resumed her seat, perhaps embarrassed. And perhaps embarrassed for me too. This might be good. I returned to my chair and leaned on my desk with some authority. "What do you do?" I said. "I mean, besides have money?"

"You resent my money?"

"No. I resent not having any."

"I'm a librarian at the downtown public library."

"Hmm, I'm impressed. I could never find my way around a library. In my half semester of college, I always got confused in the library."

"Joe, may I call you Joe?"

"Sure."

"My sister, remember?"

"Right. OK. So here's what we've got to go on. Your sister has supposedly been kidnapped, and they want $200,000 or they'll kill her; they, of course, being the Druid cult. We've got the drop-off instructions for the ransom, and all we have to do is deliver the money and Brittany will be set free and we'll all live happy lives after that. Right?"

"Then you'll do it?"

"Absolutely, that's what they pay me for."

"Would two thousand be sufficient for the job?"

"Absolutely. And I assure you, I do tithe on that."

# CHAPTER EIGHT

There was a lot of space between the seconds on the afternoon of my fast, Day 2, as I reflected on Bertie's morning visit to my office and on all that had happened in the last few days. And was I wasting my life as a gumshoe? And more than that, was America, the land of the free and the home of the brave, wasting its life, consuming, consuming, consuming? Maybe America needed to go on a fast. If I could do it, then why not the whole country? Stop unessential consumption for twenty-one days. No. It wouldn't work. All that stuff would begin to pile up on the shore and then spill over into the oceans and float back to the third-world countries where most of it was made.

And what about Brittany? Was she the bad Druid it looked like she was, swindling her mother and sister, or was there some other explanation? So there I sat, no food in my future, in Seattle, clueless. Or was there a clue, something I'd missed, something so obvious it was hard to see, something that would shine light on the whole mess?

But all I had was an empty valise. I'd left the bananas for the monkeys. What I wouldn't have given for one of those bananas now. But there was no sense dwelling on lost opportunities. I needed to retrace my steps.

There was the First Church of the Manifest Presence and Associate Pastor Bernard. Yes, I needed to pay him a little visit. And I'd almost forgotten—lost as I was in the ennui of the empty gut. What about the Spelunkers and the gun and the conspiracy evidence in my safe? I probably should have thrown it all into Puget Sound, and maybe I would yet, because who would believe such a tale, even though I did have the papers? Nobody. You could find more invent- ive plots than the Spelunkers' on the Internet, and it didn't matter that this one just happened to be true. The boys downtown would throw me out of the station if I took it to them, but what about the FBI and the CIA? No use—they were only letters to me.

Suddenly the door to my office opened and two men in black entered, the first one flashing his badge. Uh, oh. The Feds.

"They're in the safe," I said, standing to get the gun and brief- case.

"What's in the safe?" Clone 1 said.

"The Spelunkers conspiracy papers and the gun," I said. "Isn't that what you came for?"

"You ought to do something about your breath," Clone 2 said.

Clone 1 said, "We're looking for Brittany Mulligan."

"No kidding," I said, "I'm looking for her too. She took me for twenty grand."

"Eh?" Clone 1 said, looking over at Clone 2. "If you've got a complaint, son . . . we just want to ask her a few questions about a friend of hers. One King Canute, head of a group called the Latter- day Druids. He's wanted for illegal entry into the country."

So there really was a head Druid after all. Maybe Brittany had only fallen in with bad company, and now she really was kidnapped. I would search that out later, but now, even though these guys were the Feds, I knew I had to maintain my client's confidentiality no matter what.

"I haven't got a clue where Brittany is. I haven't seen her for several days, but if I do, I'll call you immediately. A person in my position likes to maintain good working relations with the FBI."

Clone 1 looked quizzically at Clone 2.

"We're plain clothes Mounties," he said.

"Right, sure. I'll be in touch."

"Eh?" Clone 1 said sharply.

"Yes, sir," I said.

Clone 2 sternly handed me his card. Without another word, the pair left my office where I was left to contemplate further this latest development in the case, a case I would later file—for many reasons, some obscure, some not—under M for "Missing, The Case of the." Then the thought struck me: How had the Feds traced Brittany to me? Ah, simple. They'd probably been talking to Associate Pastor Bernard. Bertie and her mother wouldn't have told them anything, not with the Druid threat of a dead Brittany if they ratted to the police.

So, the head Druid, King Canute, was in the country illegally. But where was he from? Where did he call home? With a name like Canute, he might have been from Britain, especially with a first name like King, although there were other Kings now, like Martin Luther King or B. B. King or Nat King Cole or King Creole or Elvis the King; these days you didn't have to be royalty to have the name King. This was a democracy, and a darned good one at that. Here anyone could be a King or a Queen for that matter, and Kings could even be Queens, and Queens Kings, as long as they worked hard and kept their noses clean; that was all that counted in this land of opportunity, where it didn't matter what the color of your skin was or whether you were born in the slums or in the lap of luxury. You were an American, and that's all that mattered.

There was no finer place in the world to be. Where else could a person be both a Christian and a private eye? A lot of countries in the world didn't even allow Christians, let alone private detectives, but in America you could be both, and nobody would deny you the right.

Yes, this was America, where a Christian detective could ply his trade without the slightest interference. And so what if there was the occasional disdainful comment from narrow-minded Christians, and who cared about the odd snicker from the unsaved? These were trivial prices to pay compared to the freedom to live the life of your choosing. Yes, here I was, Joe LaFlam, a Christian private detective following his American dream. God bless America, eh?

Then again, was it all worth it? Here I sat, hungry. And I wasn't only hungry; I was mad. I was mad that I'd fallen for the old top-off-the-ransom trick, and I was mad that I'd vowed to fast on clear fluids for another nineteen and a half days. And I was mad that I was starving and that my nerves were jumping and that my hollow gut echoed the sound of an empty life consumed by self and the driving need to acquire wealth, so that I might support a wife and have the kids and the grandkids and the registered retirement savings plans to retire on, so that I wouldn't end up in the gutter, living under tinfoil or cardboard or maybe only newspaper and the wife dead in disgrace and the kids ashamed to visit me in the desolate alley of my discontent.

Tapping sounds snapped my thoughts back from the brink. They were coming from the fingers of my left hand, thrumming the desktop. Ah, well, things weren't that bad after all. There was Bertie. Yes, I had to keep focused. I had to see her now the way I would in about three weeks. And I had to get to the bottom of Brittany's game. If I could solve the mystery and get Brittany back, I would be on easy street, or at least I would be in nineteen and a half days, when I broke my fast with a little pulp in my juice, and then my good old colon would begin to crank over again.

My right hand rang. I had absentmindedly left my cell phone in it. I beeped the OK button.

"Is that you, smart guy?" the Small Man rasped.

So, the baby boomer had survived. They were a resilient bunch, bless them.

"How's your heart?" I asked sincerely.

"Way better than yours is gonna be, smart guy. The cab company says you're a detective." He began to laugh, quietly, gently, like he didn't want to upset himself. "Well, I've got a case for you. My briefcase and my gun are missing." He laughed quietly some more.

I began to sweat. I said, "I could possibly arrange for them to be returned in exchange for—"

"Don't even think about it. Listen."

"Yeah."

"No. Listen."

"Listen to what?"

"Can't you hear?"

Suddenly I did hear. I heard heavy footsteps thump speedily down the hall and stop at my door. I stifled the urge to run. The door opened. A bead of sweat, brimming with fasting toxins, paused thoughtfully on my brow and then purposefully descended, trickling down the side of my nose.

"You still there, smart guy," the Small Man chuckled, "or are you dead?"

"Shh," I said and hung up, as I slipped stealthily beneath my desk.

From below the seat of my authority, I waited for my assassin's next move. I pulled out my piece, my trusty .22, and held my breath. And then I heard it, something familiar, something I had heard quite recently. It was a sound, a muffled gasping sound, and then choking and then gagging and then a major thump, as something very large hit the floor of my office.

I was trained to be careful. I needed to survive, if only to lead at least one person to the Lord before I died. That was something I had never done, and there was hardly anyone I knew who had led someone to the Lord either. Why was that?

I peered over the top of my desk. In a lump lay a mound of a man in a blue suit. Above his chubby cheeks his temples were graying. Another baby boomer with a bad ticker. Those boomers were falling like flies. I maneuvered carefully to his side and kicked his .30-millimeter toward my safe. My cell rang again.

"Yes," I whispered.

"Is that you, smart guy? You're supposed to be dead."

"Your sidekick doesn't look so good. He must have run up the stairs." I checked his pulse. He was still in the land of the living.

I said, "He must be twenty kilos overweight. When will you ever learn?"

"How much is twenty kilos, smart guy?"

"About forty-five pounds."

"That's hardly anything."

"You must be lonely down there. Looks like your associate will be down to see you in an ambulance soon."

"Don't get too smart, smart guy," he said, exciting himself. "I guarantee real soon you're going to be a dead smart guy and then you won't be such a smart guy, will you?"

"Bless you. As a Christian I only hope you and your colleague here reform your lives and come to the knowledge of the truth. Now you must excuse me; I need to dial 9-1-1."

"A Christian? A Christian? You're a Christian? What kind of Christian steals a man's briefcase and gun and leaves him to die in the hospital? You Christians are all alike. A bunch of hypocrites. And I bet you think telling me you're a Christian changes things. Well, it doesn't; I'm going to kill you anyway, only now I'm going to enjoy killing you even more."

"Don't excite yourself. Your heart, remember?"

I beeped him off and beeped on again to dial 9-1-1. The guy's face on the floor was gray. I checked his pulse. His heart was still pumping.

"Hello, yes, I've got an emergency . . . a coronary, I think. Send an ambulance to 666 Marlon, Suite 316."

"What's your name, sir?"

"Joe. Joe LaFlam. Christian detective."

"LaFlam at 666 Marlon?"

"Yes, that's right."

"316?"

"Right."

"It's on the way."

I looked at the heavy man on the floor and shook my head.

"The poor baby boomers. They got addicted to fat and caffeine and most any other substance that wasn't good for them, and now they suffer. Their poor hearts have begun to give out. They consumed the resources and plundered the country and now we'll have to pay, you and I. Yes, they indulged, and now guys like you and me end up with nothing. And not only that, I'm not eating either. I'm fasting, so that He might hear from on high, and then I might finally make something of my life and find a good wife."

"Would you get off the line, sir?"

# CHAPTER NINE

The day began slowly. In my bed I stared at my digital alarm clock. The time was long from one minute to the next. I knew this was bound to be the killer day, as the remaining, most stubborn toxins were hounded out from their fleshly hiding places. That's what *The Fast Life* said. Day 3 was the killer.

But I had to get out of bed. The ransom had to be delivered. And I needed to execute my plan, a plan that was guaranteed to solve the case, recover my inheritance, and put the bad guys behind bars where they belonged. And I would get the girl. And yes, King Canute would soon be history. I raised myself on my elbow and swung my feet out. It was cold. That was another thing the book said. When you were fasting, you were burning low-grade fuel, mostly stored fat and other nonessentials, which left you feeling colder than normal. And my fingers were thinning slightly. I was losing weight. I didn't have that much to lose either. What would happen if I ran out of fuel before the three weeks were up? *The Fast Life* had said not to worry; there was always more waste to burn, for forty days anyway, but after that your body would begin to starve to death; it would then sort of eat itself up.

And you had to be careful breaking the fast because if you weren't careful something bad might happen. I remembered a woman in the church who was fond of telling a fasting story. A person she knew broke a long fast with a big bowl of chili, and according to this woman, this person's intestines sort of looped over themselves in the shock of it all and tied themselves in a knot. The person had

to have surgery to get her insides untied, or so the story went. By
the look of her, the woman who told the story hadn't missed many
meals in her life, but still it was a good warning. I envisioned eating
a bowl of chili for about a minute and then, realizing I was freezing,
got dressed and went downstairs. There was no time to pray.

"Up and at 'em, eh?" my mother said. She was sitting on her
usual perch at the kitchen table.

"Think we could turn the heat up a bit?" I said, sitting down.

"It'll pass dear. Don't worry." She went to the fridge, poured
some red juice into a glass, and then set it front of me.

"Clamato," she said, pleased with her choice of the clam and
tomato beverage.

"Great," I said, smelling the fishy liquid, "but I'm supposed to
drink only clear fluids," and then, desperate, I gulped some down.

"Are you going to the office today, dear?"

"Yeah," I said, focused on my upcoming ordeal, "I've got a ransom to deliver."

"Ransom? You mean you're involved in a kidnapping? Do the
police know?"

"Never mind, I shouldn't have mentioned anything. You know
my cases are confidential."

"A bit testy on this fast are we, dear? Never mind. Finish your
clam juice. It'll give you strength."

I drank the rest of it, wondering what part of the clam produced it.

Downtown, in my office, because there was no one else to ask,
I impatiently questioned the wall as to why the worst fast day just
had to coincide with a hard work day. I didn't want to ask Him
and risk sounding like I was grumbling. Grumbling or not, I was
nauseated; the clam juice was disagreeing with my stomach, and I
also had a hunch it was going to pass on through my system rapidly
and not too politely. I waited for Bertie, concerned that my clam
breath would be worse than yesterday's stomach fumes. I squirted,

feeling depressed and losing confidence in my plan to solve the case and win the girl. Who did I think I was anyway, Angela Lansbury? Oh, what did it matter? The stage was set. My plan would go ahead, regardless of whether it would succeed.

There was a knock at the door and in hurried Bertie, carrying a valise. I stood to greet her as she slid the money onto my desk.

"Well, here it is," she said. "Two hundred thousand in small bills."

She opened the valise, and I peered inside.

"Petty cash," I said in my best Humphrey Bogart impression, admiring the greenbacks and good-naturedly fighting off the depression hunger brings.

"Who are you trying to be?" Bertie asked.

"Humphrey Bogart," I said, hurt.

"Oh," she said, and then sniffing, asked, "What smells like dead fish?"

"Breakfast," I said, annoyed and then brazenly shot two squirts in.

"I thought you were not supposed to eat . . . oh, never mind. Are you ready to deliver the ransom? It's all in order."

"As ready as I'll ever be."

"That doesn't sound too encouraging."

"I'm just a little down this morning, what with this kidnapping business and then there's the Spelunker conspirators, and two of them in the hospital with heart conditions, and who are they going to send next to kill me, and what about King Canute?"

"Spelunkers? What could cave explorers possibly conspire about, and why would they want to kill you?"

"It's a long story, sister; I'll bore you with it sometime. Meanwhile, I've got a ransom to deliver."

"Are you sure you're OK?" she said, again unimpressed with my Bogart impersonation.

"What difference does that make? I've got a job to do. And when duty calls, that's all that's important in this game. You don't lie down just because a little adversity comes your way. You stand up for what's right. You do your duty. You fulfill your calling. Today it's delivering a ransom, and tomorrow, saving the nations of the world from being forced to unite into one socialist state ruled by a one-world government with an engorged Clinton and his look-alikes heading the show."

"What are you talking about?"

"The conspiracy. I'm all that stands between us and brutal world dictatorship, where the few will rule the rest of us ruthlessly, and we in North America will no longer live lives of freedom; freedom to work where we choose, to live where we choose, to speak politically correctly, to assemble, to invest in the stock market and in retirement plans so we don't end up graying in an alley, sleeping with the dumpsters. No, their insidious plan is to take our freedoms away. They're numbing us now so we will accept their plan without question. They're entertaining us and drugging us and World-Wide-Webbing us and teaching us to see the world as our only hope, so we will bow and scrape to preserve our puny, superficial lives and embrace peace at any cost."

"Toxins?"

"Yeah, they're bad today. *The Fast Life* says the third day is the worst."

"You have a plan?"

"Yeah, but it's best you don't know."

"I'll go with you to the park."

"No, please, you go home and stay with your mother. This is my work; this is detective work. That's what they pay me for."

"Take care of yourself . . . and the money," she said.

Bertie came around to my side of the desk and kissed me on the cheek. I must not have smelled like clams anymore.

"Ah, Clamato," she said.

"Only eighteen days to go," I replied.

# CHAPTER TEN

I had the money, I would get the girl. I had the money, I would get the girl. I had the money, I would get the girl. That's all I had on my mind as I neared the trash can in front of the monkey cage in the park in the rain where I'd had my most recent embarrassment in the detective business. But who would know that except for the police . . . and the kidnappers, if they really were kidnappers?

Yes, I had the money and I would get the girl. All was going as planned. I was feeling more energetic, except for a little weakness in the knees. The poisons must have worked themselves out. I strode toward the trash can and boldly stuffed the valise into its gaping mouth. A couple of monkeys in their cage in the rain observed me doing the deed, then carried on with their business. I looked about me. There were a few people out for a stroll in the park in the rain, and a few joggers, pounding their fearful way through life in the rain, as if the Death Angel were licking at their heels in the rain, which he very well could have been, but who was there among us in our Western world who could see such things, mired as we were in the tyranny of our rational minds? I looked among them for any sign of suspicious behavior and, finding none, made my way out of the park and back to my car, noting as I went a gray squirrel hustling his nut up a tree in the rain in preparation for the winter.

I sat behind the wheel of my '75 Mustang, waiting in the rain. It wasn't a classic Mustang, but it ran. And that's all you needed in this life: a car that got you from A to B. Never mind all the pretension, the need for luxury, or excessive speed or glitz to impress the world or to impress the women. No, I was past all that, as I sat there with an excellent view of the trash can. I waited all afternoon and into the evening in the rain, drinking apple juice. I'd brought four liters with me to while away the time. It was good, wholesome, pure, real apple juice, squeezed from real apples, so that you had to shake the sludge off the bottom to mix it properly. I wondered if apple sludge and clam juice were in the same category.

By 10:00 P.M. there was still no sign, but the rain had stopped. Impatient, I emerged in the dry air to walk to the can in front of the monkey cage. I reached inside. The valise was gone. During the day I had only nodded off briefly, one of those nods where you're not even sure if you did nod, except when you looked at your watch and saw some time was missing. Yes, that's when they must have made the grab. It wasn't my fault. Fasting was tiring.

Or maybe they hadn't made the grab when I nodded—maybe it was during one of my trips to the park's washroom, although I was never in there long. In hindsight, the four liters of natural apple juice were probably not the best choice for a fasting stake-out. Then again it could even have happened when I used the park pay phone—having forgotten my cell at the office—to tell the dispatcher I wouldn't be driving the cab tonight. Whenever it happened, I resolved to forgive myself. As I considered my next move, the police cruiser pulled up.

"Is that you, Sherlock?" the officer said, getting out of his vehicle. "Find any bananas tonight? I hardly recognized you without your cape and the two-way hat."

I wasn't in the mood.

"No, officer, I was just on my way home."

"It's a long way to London from here. Why don't you join me in the car for a minute, Detective LaFlam, and we'll discuss again your attraction to the monkeys and that trash can."

"Yes, officer," I said. "You know best."

# CHAPTER ELEVEN

They hadn't detained me long this time. After all, there was nothing to hold me for. Examining trash cans wasn't a felony in this state or in any other state for that matter. The officer had simply been injecting some amusement into his dreary evening. I forgave him and hurried to my office to await the kidnappers' response to my brilliant strategy.

I saw it as I came down the hall. My office door. It was ajar. I pulled out my piece, nudged the door open, reached in, and turned on the light. Uh, oh . . . uh, oh. My life had ended. There it stood, its door open. My safe. The foolproof safe I had paid good, hard cash for. Empty. Yes, my life had ended. The safe was empty, and my fasting stomach was empty, too, an empty tomb in which a host of butterflies now flew. I collapsed into my chair and stared at the emptiness of it all. The Spelunker conspiracy papers were gone along with the gun. From under the loose stacks on my desk, ringing came. My cell phone was where I'd left it. I dug it out and beeped it on.

"Well, hallelujah, smart guy. I apologize for mocking you and your profession. You do pretty well for yourself. You really are a smart guy. But not as smart as me, smart guy, 'cause I've got what's mine and now I've got what's yours too."

"You got a point to make?"

"Sure, smart guy, I've got a point to make. Don't think just because you're a Christian and you've donated your life savings to my retirement that I'm not going to kill you. Because I am. Only now I'm going to enjoy killing you even more because what's a cab driver/detective doing with that kind of money unless you're working for somebody and cab driving was only a cover to steal my briefcase. Or maybe you just bilked some poor widow out of that $200,000. Either way, you're dead, Mr. Hypocrite Smart Guy."

"I hear ya."

"Well, hear this again. You're one dead Mr. Hypocrite Smart Guy."

"Bring it on," I said and beeped him off.

Yeah, at that moment I hoped he would come and finish the job. Granted, I was angry, and my response to him hadn't been very Christian, but that's what *The Fast Life* said would happen. Anger and irritability would surface as the poisons did. No, I hadn't been very Christian about his threat to kill me. I wondered if being killed for knowing about the Spelunker conspiracy would count as martyr-dom. After all, I was fasting too. No, probably not.

But I was dead now either way. The $200,000 was gone, and Bertie and Mrs. Mulligan would have my head if the Spelunkers didn't get me first. I had gambled, and that had been a bad idea. I was living proof that Christians shouldn't gamble. My first gamble was on Brittany being the culprit; and if she wasn't, she would be dead. But I reassured myself that none of my clients ever got killed in my cases, so she was pretty well guaranteed to be alive.

Yes, I was certain Brittany had been the kidnapper of herself, and finding bananas in the valise today was her just reward. She should have considered herself blessed getting them, too, because I nearly ate them myself. But if Brittany really had been kidnapped . . . no, there was no sense thinking anymore in that direction.

Content to lose myself in the depths of my trial, fatigue overtook me, and I collapsed on my office couch and succumbed to sleep.

The next morning I awoke to see an elegant, well-dressed senior, whose hair was just one shade short of pink, standing in my office. I made a mental note to make sure I locked the door in the future.

"Mr. LaFlam," she said softly.

"In the flesh," I said, covering my mouth, the inside of which felt like a cottage-cheese-textured ceiling gone bad.

"I'm Mrs. Mulligan. Faith Mulligan."

I was dead now. But strangely, I had some peace about it, and for some reason Mrs. Mulligan had a familiar smell about her. I couldn't quite place it. Where had I smelled that before?

"Yes, Mrs. Mulligan, of course. But I had expected Bertie."

Mrs. Faith Mulligan bowed her head, collapsed into my client's chair, opened her purse, took out a lace handkerchief, and began to sob. Life is misery. Was there no end?

"Bertie's . . . Bertie's gone," she said.

"Gone? Gone where?"

"First Brittany and now Bertie. Bertie's been . . . she's been . . ." she sobbed.

I pondered her synopsis and then countered.

"Don't you mean first Bertie, second Brittany, and third Bertie again?"

"Huh? What are you saying? Bertie's not been gone twice, or has she? How confusing. How am I to . . . ? Oh, maybe, are you sure? Anyway, I do know Brittany has not come back yet. Didn't you deliver the ransom? Brittany should have come home by now if you delivered the ransom."

I shook my head at life's twists. I'd really done it this time. But I couldn't bring myself to tell her that the ransom was now lining a Spelunker's pockets and that her daughter Brittany was a felon.

Hoping to spare her the worst, I said, "I don't want you to think the worst, but kidnappers can't be trusted."

"Aaaaaaahhhhhhhh!" Mrs. Faith Mulligan screamed, and then recommenced sobbing.

She fumbled in her purse and threw a note across my desk. It contained those now familiar words: "IF YOU DON'T FOLLOW DIRECTIONS TO A TEE, OR IF YOU RAT TO THE POLICE, WE

WILL SACRIFICE YOUR LOVED ONE, BERTIE MULLIGAN, TO THE DRUID GOD. SINCERELY, YOUR HEAD DRUID, KING CANUTE."

"So," I said, "they strike again."

"Strike again? What kind of man are you? King Canute is going to sacrifice Bertie to the Druid god, and Brittany's not come home yet. She could be . . . she could be . . . ohhh . . . what kind of a Christian are you?"

Good question. Well, at least I knew what kind I wasn't. I wasn't the kind to dwell in the past. What was done, was done, and that's all there was to it. I was down $20,000; Mrs. Faith Mulligan was down $280,000, or was she only down $200,000? Anyway, it was all relative. And my loss was relatively as big as hers. She could afford it. If she had to, she could simply sell a hotel. And there was no real sense telling her that her $200,000 hadn't gone to kidnappers but to ease the retirement of a Spelunker conspirator. Such information would only have clouded the issue. Her money had gone to criminals; that's all Mrs. Faith Mulligan needed to know.

But aside from the money, she was also no doubt thinking there was a possibility she'd lost two daughters. But that was relative also. I was the real loser there too. If Brittany and Bertie had indeed been sacrificed, I was out two wives. What was worse? As their husband, I would have known them longer in the long run, so in the long run, I was potentially the one most aggrieved. But the truth was they were both still alive because I was almost certain none of my clients ever died in my cases.

"Well," she repeated accusingly and sobbed, "what kind are you?"

"I'm a born-again Christian, Mrs. Mulligan. Is there any other kind?"

"Well, I'm Baptist and we Baptists don't go for any of this loosey-goosey kind of Christianity. You're probably one of those charismatics, aren't you? No respect for decency and order. Well, I tell you, you'd better find my girls real soon. If not, you'll be singing that gibberish of yours with your hands raised, all right, as they march you off to jail."

"I see King Canute wants a cool million this time."

"I really don't like your attitude."

"Forgive me. However, it's my duty now as an ethical Christian detective to recommend you go to the police."

"Police? You see what the note says. We can't risk that."

"We? It's 'we' again, is it? Well, sure, why not . . . ? No, you're right, Mrs. Mulligan, we can't risk it. I guess it's you and me now, Mrs. Mulligan."

"And don't forget there's Pen."

"Pen? Who's Pen?"

"Penelope. My youngest."

"You have another one?"

"Yes, of course, you didn't know? I thought you were a detective."

"Hmm."

"So what are we going to do now, Mr. LaFlam?"

"Any sons?"

"What possible relevance could that have now?"

"Have you got a million handy?"

"I can get it."

"Get it and bring it here tomorrow morning about ten. I'll make the delivery."

"That's it? You'll make the delivery?"

"Don't worry, I've got a plan, and a lot of ransom-delivery experience to back it up. Incidentally, you do have the full million, don't you?"

"Yes, of course, and I'll be bringing my chauffeur with me, who's also my bodyguard."

"So then why don't you just have your bodyguard deliver the ransom?"

"It's not in his job description. Oh, you mean . . . I see . . . would five thousand cover your fee?"

"Sorry, I wasn't hinting . . . uh, would that be in advance?"

"Yes, perhaps I can arrange that."

"Fine. I don't mean to be pushy, but I'm still owed three thousand for the last ransom delivery fee."

"OK, eight thousand, but how can you be so callous when my daughters have been kidnapped? Don't you care about them at all?"

"Yes, I care, though I don't know why I should. I've tried to be the best detective I can be in this case. I've been compassionate. I've followed the rules. I even donated my inheritance to save Bertie."

"What do you mean? Bertie hasn't been saved yet."

"Oh, that's right, I guess you weren't in on that one. I wonder where Brittany got the $80,000. Never mind, when you give me eight I'll only be down twelve."

"You're a strange man. I don't know why Bertie hired you in the first place."

"It was actually Brittany who hired me in the first place, but don't bother yourself about that. Just have the money here tomorrow, and I'll make sure you get your daughters back and your money, or my name isn't Joe LaFlam. And do us all a favor and keep an eye on Penelope."

Mrs. Faith Mulligan exited my office. My phone rang, and I beeped it on. It was Mother.

"I know you're not eating, but are you coming home, John? I'm worried, what with you talking about a kidnapping, and now you not coming home all night."

"I told you not to call me that when I'm at the office, Mother."

"You're a strange one, dear. And may I remind you that Doe is a good honest name too. And while I'm on the subject, it's not healthy for you to be living in Seattle in your mind either."

"Please, Mother, not now. It's been a hard day."

"Well?"

"Yes, OK, I'll come home and watch you eat lunch."

"No sense being nasty, dear. This fasting business was your idea, remember?"

I beeped the phone and slumped on my desk. It wasn't my fault. John Doe was simply not a name for a dynamic private detective such as myself. If I'd known my father, it might have been a different story. But the way things were now . . . oh, well, what did it matter? He was gone, and that was all I needed to know.

The case was the important thing, and right now what I really needed to know was who was doing what to whom and for what reason. Was money really the motive? It usually was. But in this crazy, mixed-up case of kidnappings, who knew? Anything might have been possible. Still, Mrs. Faith Mulligan seemed on the up-and-up, and Bertie, too, but who could be sure? And Brittany, well, I was sure she was up to no good. But why? I was pretty well certain nobody had really been kidnapped, except maybe for Bertie the second time. And the only money missing was my twenty grand and of course Bertie's and Mrs. Mulligan's two hundred Gs, since neither of them seemed to know about the first eighty thousand.

Yes, given the evidence, it all pointed to a pretty slippery Brittany and her accomplice King Canute. But why? For the money? She was an heiress not an hairdresser. I would have liked to have seen her and King's faces when they opened the valise full of bananas. But then my holding back the two hundred thousand had only made her mad, mad enough to kidnap her sister Bertie for real the second time and mad enough to up the ante to a cool million.

And, surprise, surprise, there just happened to be a youngest daughter too: Penelope. How did she figure into the picture? These were all questions I knew I had to answer, and I would when I got to the bottom of it all. That is, if the Spelunkers didn't get me first.

# CHAPTER TWELVE

$B$ack at the house, I said a few reassuring words to my mother about the kidnapping case, knocked back a glass of Clamato and offered the obligatory apology, once again, for changing my name.

"To protect the innocent," I joked lamely.

"Oh, that's fine, dear," she said. "And don't worry, you're not a failure."

I received her consoling words and carried them with me to my room. Despite Day 4's rough beginning with Mrs. Mulligan, I now felt peaceful and not really hungry; I would have eaten something if I weren't fasting, but I wasn't desperate for food. Yes, I had way more peace than that. I wasn't just free from desperation; I was truly content. I lay on my bed, took out my Bible, and began to read Proverbs. There was a lot of wisdom in there.

After a chapter or two, I stopped reading and began to meditate on recent events. And then the thought came again that perhaps I was in the wrong business. And maybe God was trying to tell me something. And maybe, heaven forbid, I was fasting for the wrong reasons. Sure, I was denying my flesh, but with the intention of feeding it later, if and when my petitions were answered. Was that legitimate? My motives for the fast seemed to be centered on my needs only. But *The Fast Life* emphasized that the fasting discipline was to be selfless not selfish, and that you were supposed to inter-cede for others, especially for the lost.

Examining my thoughts, I noticed Day 4 was becoming much too serious. Yes, to carry on I needed to be more lighthearted. But *The Fast Life* had warned this would happen. Spiritual reality would become sharper. Was I ready for that? God only knew. But I was afraid to talk to Him about it.

I almost always preferred to keep Him at a distance, and only read Scripture now and then, and, of course, listen to my pastor preach, though he wasn't a natural at it. That way there would be fewer demands on my life because, after all, Scripture was hard to follow and you couldn't be held accountable for what you didn't quite understand. Some Scripture, of course, was quite straightforward, but there again, how many Christians really followed even that much?

No, it was too risky to ask God directly what He wanted me to do. It was easier to ask Him for things—like a wife, for instance. No harm in that. And maybe He would straighten out this kidnapping case too. Yes, there was nothing wrong with asking Him to bless my chosen profession and also get me a wife.

I snapped out of my meditation in the nick of time, before I lapsed into a spiritual conversation with God. Yes, fasting certainly did increase spiritual perception. But how desirable was that in America in the new millennium? Kingdom principles lacked a certain compatibility with the present order of things in the land of the free. Perhaps I would talk to Him about that predicament some other time. But right now I didn't have time to pray; it was imperative that I go down to visit the First Church of the Manifest Presence and talk to Associate Pastor Bernard.

The trip downtown was uneventful except for the sense I had of the world floating by and of my having an intense appreciation for all the good things in it. My Mustang especially gave me great pleasure, and I was thankful for it. Yes, I was thankful for a lot of things. My health, for instance, and my mother and my church, though I might soon leave it. And food, how wonderful it was, from the humble leaf of lettuce to the exalted T-bone. All of it was good and would be delectable in seventeen days, when I again put on the old feed bag. But now I was in no hurry for the fast days to end; I was beginning to savor hunger; I appreciated for the first time lacking something I wanted.

A horn sounded; I had been meditating on a green light.

"Same to . . . I mean, bless you, sir."

Blissful, I continued on down to the church to meet Associate Pastor Bernard with bubbles of joy welling up for no apparent reason. It was unbelievable. Here I was, responsible for the Mulligans' missing money and the Spelunkers had vowed to kill me. I was wifeless, and without dramatic, supernatural intervention, I really didn't have a future in this life, but I was a happy man. Nothing could touch me. I had a deep, eternal sense of being saved. It was awesome, even though the use of that word sickened me.

Inside the First Church of the Manifest Presence, a.k.a. the Guide Hall, I saw Associate Pastor Bernard sitting in a circle with other members of his flock. I recognized the elderly Chicken Man, even though he sported a green jumpsuit today, and the pogo-sticker was there, too, along with four or five others. Bernard saw me and waved for me to join the group. I reluctantly obliged and sat down, sensing the circle of believers covertly assess me.

"We're doing street ministry today, Joe," Bernard said. "Would you like to join us?"

A few in the group shuffled their feet and shifted in their chairs, obviously waiting for my reaction and no doubt wondering whether I would affirm them and help relieve their insecurity concerning the mission ahead or reject them as idle dreamers and delusional in their zealotry. But no, Joe LaFlam wouldn't let them down.

"Sure," I said, aware my voice twanged with bravado, "I love to witness."

I immediately questioned my motive for lying. Had I lied to encourage them or to hide my fear of appearing to lack commit-

ment? And was lying in such circumstances a sin? On the scale of
things, it was probably not as bad as making copies of copyrighted
Christian music tapes, which I never did, though I knew some who
did, including my pastor. And was that a good enough excuse to
leave my church if I needed to? People left churches for less cause
than that.

Of course, a person needed a reason to leave, and I probably
would leave if things worked out with Brittany, which didn't seem
likely since she more than likely was a felon. But if Bertie were the
one, then she might just fit into my more conservative church and
I would stay although I was beginning to feel drawn to this more
charismatic expression of the faith, though I wasn't exactly certain
why. And if that were the case, I would have to leave my conservative church, and, if Bertie were the one, she would just have to go
along because, of course, the man was the head of the household
and always knew best about these things. And as far as leaving my
church went, I wouldn't need to have a reason to leave because it
was a free country and people could come and go as they pleased.
After all, the Church was run as a democracy, and wasn't that how
our Lord intended it to be?

"You all right?" Bernard asked.

I snapped out of it and realized I had been entranced, staring at
the floor and speeding in my mind. That was another hazard I had
read about in *The Fast Life*. One was prone to speed in one's mind,
with one thought following another until the chemicals in one's
brain reached equilibrium and it stopped.

"I'm sorry," I said. "I'm on a twenty-one-day fast, and not a
Daniel one either, but the clear-juice kind, except for, I cannot tell
a lie, the odd glass of Clamato, which is, I believe, borderline, the
degree of transgression depending on where the clam juice actually
comes from and how much pulp is in the tomato juice. My mother's
fault, really; she caught me in a weak moment, which, I've noticed,
is most of the time, so I've fallen to Clamato temptation several

times since. I'm lonely, you see. I've never married, but I know
God understands because, of course, He understands everything.
And as you know, He came to set us free from bondage, so why sink
into deep guilt and despair, which isn't from God, when forgiveness
can be so easily received? Clamato, shlamato—why sweat the small
stuff? Don't you agree?"

They seemed to be a quiet group. They looked at one another
inquiringly, no doubt to seek consensus concerning my question.

"Well," Bernard said finally, asserting his leadership, "I suppose
we should get started. And, uh, Joe, why don't you just stay close to
me, and I can fill you in on our mission plan as we go."

"Swell," I said, "I've got a few questions for you."

As we headed for the great outdoors, I suddenly liked Bernard.
And I noticed for the first time he glowed. He was a real saint. But
was I letting my recently attained spiritual acuity influence my professional judgment? I needed to keep my purpose for being here front and
center, and that purpose was to find a clue to the whole kidnapping
madness that was King Canute and the Mulligans. What an adventure
life was. And then there was young Penelope. Hmm. Was it possible?

We left the Guide Hall and headed out on our adventure into
the realm of witnessing. What a life. I had come to talk to Bernard
about Brittany, and now here I was serving the Lord. What a transition. Every day held the thrill of new possibilities. Why had I been
so rut-bound that I hadn't been able to enjoy life to the fullest?
Yes, hunger brought life into perspective, a true perspective, where
service to the poor, the homeless, the downtrodden was the order
of the day. How remote the Mulligans and the Spelunkers seemed
to me now; they inhabited a far different world than this one, a
world in which it didn't matter who you were, whether you were a
Presbyterian, a Catholic, a Methodist, or a Jew, as long as you had
the courage to share your convictions.

Hmm, "a Jew" didn't quite fit into that list; if you were Jewish,
you were more than likely born that way, except for those who

were converts to Judaism, and naturally they weren't Christians then unless they converted again, and then they probably wouldn't become Christians but Messianic Jews. But if a person, a Gentile say, simply wanted to know Jesus, he could skip that middle stage of converting to Judaism first and simply become a Christian right away. And for those who were born Jewish, well, they were unlikely to give the Christian faith the time of day, given the atrocities committed against them under the crusading banner of. . . .

"We're giving out sandwiches to the homeless today," Bernard said, gesturing toward his and the others' backpacks, as we headed down the nearest alley.

"Isn't that ironic since I'm fasting?" I said.

Bernard nodded, and then I remembered I wasn't supposed to tell others I was fasting. It had something to do with the choice of receiving your reward now or much later. So if I chose to get recognition now, in eternity I would lose my reward for my twenty-one days. I hoped I hadn't mentioned my fast enough to lose all my reward for the last four days. After all, it was hard to keep your mouth shut when all around you people were continually obsessed with food. But I was above all that now. I resolved to extend grace to my more fleshly companions.

The group began to spread out down the alley as they encountered here a person, there a person, one under cardboard, another fishing in a dumpster. Wherever they found them, they handed out the sandwiches from their packs. Bernard gave me a few sandwiches from his stash, and I eagerly sought my first encounter with the filthy, hungry, lost souls of the alley. I hardly noticed I held food in my hands; I was now a living, fasting sacrifice on a mission. I felt my knees go jelly up when I approached two legs sticking out from behind a graffiti-emblazoned dumpster. Bending over, sandwich in hand, I sought the torso and head.

"What er you looking at, boy?" a voice said from the shadows.

"Uh, I brought you a sandwich."

"What, you my mother? I suppose it's time to get up and go to school."

He sat up. "Abner?" I said.

"Well, if it isn't the private eye. Hot on the trail of the bad guys, I suppose."

"What are you doing here?"

"Where am I supposed to be?"

"You're a Christian now, Abner. You're a new man, not a drunk in an alley."

"Look who's talking. You're still a private eye, ain't ya?"

"Come on, I'll help you up."

Abner allowed me to give him a hand up. He smelled bad.

He said, "You better do something about your breath, boy."

I was shocked. Finding Abner behind the dumpster had truly surprised me. I'd gone out to help deliver sandwiches to the street people, and instead I'd found a real person.

"What happened?" I said, as Abner began eating the egg salad with his dirty hands.

"Deviled egg. Figures," he muttered.

"Why are you backsliding, Abner?"

"Tired of you people," he said with his mouth full. "Yer not real. I was just yer pet bum."

"You shouldn't judge the message because the messengers aren't perfect." Even I was encouraged by my insight. I wondered where it had come from.

"Perfect? Yer all plastic. Look at ya. A private detective. If I got the Bible message right, the mystery's already been solved."

I was happy to see Bernard coming over to help me.

"You know this man?" Bernard asked.

"Yeah, he's a member of our church."

"Was," Abner said, beginning on the second egg sandwich.

"Bernard," I said, "maybe the church could help Abner out with a place to stay."

"We are the church," Bernard said.

Hmm, this outreach business was coming a little too close to home.

"But I'm not trained like you," I offered lamely.

"See?" Abner said. "I'm just an experiment to you do-gooders."

"It doesn't all depend on us," Bernard said, admonishing Abner. "You have to make a few good choices yourself."

"If I could've done that thirty years ago, I wouldn't need nothin' now," Abner said.

I suddenly felt a surge in my heart to be a sheep and not a goat.

"I'll take him," I said to Bernard. "I'll look after him."

"You talkin' about me, Mr. Private Eye, like I was nothin' standin' here. Yer gonna take care of me? Who's gonna take care o' you?"

Bernard said, "You can only help him if he wants to be helped."

"Yer no Mother Teresa, are ya?" Abner said to Bernard. "Oh, who needs ya? I'm tired of ya all." Abner turned to resume his position behind the dumpster.

"Come on, Abner," I said. "Let's go to my car." To Bernard I said, "I'll catch up . . . I still need to ask you a few questions."

I hustled Abner away in the direction of my car, though he wasn't in the mood to be rushed. He was hungover and his balance unsteady, his joints still stiff from his sojourn in the alley. He chose to lie in the backseat and promised to wait there while I returned to see Bernard.

"You private eyes is all the same" were his parting words.

I found Bernard and his disciples one alley over, handing out their sandwiches. He agreed to answer some questions about Brittany as we walked.

"Shoot," he said.

"How long have you known Brittany?"

"Is Brittany in trouble?" he said.

"I don't know for sure."

"Last time we talked, her sister had been kidnapped, and you were helping her out. Where's Brittany now? I haven't seen her for a few days. And why haven't we heard anything about her sister?"

"I thought I was asking the questions."

I was getting hungry again, and my earlier euphoria was wearing thin. I needed a rest.

"Well?" Bernard said.

"Brittany's missing, Bertie's missing, the money's missing; Mrs. Faith Mulligan's not happy, and not only that, she's got another daughter. Where will it all end?"

"I think you better pray, brother."

"Yeah." I was beginning to sink further.

"Yeah, what?"

"Yeah, I pray that the end is near."

"It's not yet," Bernard said, waxing eschatological. "The church isn't ready. We're not without spot or wrinkle, that's for sure."

"Then what about the Rapture?"

"This isn't the time or place to get into a discussion about the Rapture. We shouldn't major on the minors anyway. All we have to agree on is that the Lord is coming back."

"What do you mean? If we're going to get raptured, then I want to know. If we're going to get zapped right on out of here, I'm not going to do this fast, that's for sure. What would be the point? You'd think you experts could get it straight, so simple Christians like me would know one way or the other. Why go through a lot of blood, sweat, and tears if—zappo—we get hoisted out of here before anything bad happens. What are you talking about, major on the minors? It's not minor. Here one day, gone tomorrow. You think that's minor?"

"Are these the questions you wanted to ask me?"

"What could be more important than the Rapture? If Brittany and Bertie really are Christians, which they say they are, and tonight's the Rapture, we'll all meet the Lord in the air and that'll be it, case solved."

"I wouldn't count on that happening tonight. And try to take it easy, LaFlam. The fasting's going to your head."

"OK, I hear you." I tried to calm myself with a couple of deep breaths and then said, "OK, I'm fine, really . . . I'm OK, I'm all right, yes, I'm all together now. So, do you know why Brittany started coming to your church?"

"She said she wanted to put a little distance between herself and the rest of her family. And she didn't feel she fit in with her family's church anymore."

"Did you ever meet Bertie or her mother or Pen?"

"Pen?"

"Penelope, the youngest."

"No, just Brittany. She's been coming about six months. And she's sincere."

"Sure, I'd like to believe she's sincere, but I really think she's been taking us all for a ride. She's behind the kidnappings, and not only that, I think she's in partnership with this Canute character, the head of the Latter-day Druids."

"Brittany? I don't think so. That's pretty hard to believe."

"Yeah, well, I didn't think a lot of things until recently, and now conspirators are trying to kill me because I found out about their plot to unite North America and the world under one socialist government controlled by a rich elite."

"Everybody knows that. Why would they want to kill you for knowing that?"

"Ah, but have you heard of the Spelunkers?"

"You mean people who explore caves? What do they have to do with anything?"

"See, you don't know the whole deal. But I do, and that's why they want to kill me."

"Sure . . . look, I've got some people to feed. Anymore questions?"

"Yeah, if you're the associate, who's the senior pastor? I haven't seen him around."

"He's on stress leave."

"How long's he been off?"

"Uh, about two . . . yeah, two months. I'm holding down the fort till he comes back, if he does."

"He might not?"

"Who knows? Pastoring takes its toll."

"Do you know where he is?"

"He was going to visit relatives on Vancouver Island for awhile, I think."

"Oh, up in Canada, eh?"

"What?"

"Never mind, it's great country, even though it's mostly ice and snow this time of year."

"There's no snow—"

"All right, I better see how Abner's doing. Thanks for your help."

I hurried back to my car. I needed to get to my office and sow some seeds. The solution to the mystery was beginning to fall into place now. What first seemed to be imponderable, given the bizarre circumstances surrounding the kidnappings, was now starting to yield a snapshot, as pieces of the rapidly developing negative formed a loose mosaic of bright, shifting possibilities that now lit the way for my brain, and, indeed, my ever-more holy, fasting mind, to envision the enormity of the crime. In other words, the jig was quite possibly up.

Abner moaned when I started my Mustang. He lay hugging himself and shivering, his face wedged into the back of the seat. I decided to take him to my office for the afternoon and then figure out what to do with him next. I wasn't much good at hospitality and selfless servanthood, and God only knew why I had volunteered for this kind of duty today.

Once in the parking garage, I rousted Abner out of his stupor. I was thankful he was in good enough shape to climb the stairs. He made it as far as my office couch, where he resumed hugging himself and shivering, his face again wedged in for security.

His muffled grumble said, "Twenty-four hours . . . to sweat it out. Find a lost kitten or somethin' while you're waitin'." And then he added almost inaudibly, "And thanks. Maybe you private eyes ain't all the same after all."

I threw a blanket over him and then took up my position behind my desk. I then realized he had made the decision to dry out all by himself, which was a pretty good sign, all things considered. Maybe he had decided to return to the fold. But the question was, would I? Was I going to go to my church on Sunday? I was beginning to have my doubts. But if I did go, would they notice how thin I was getting? And would I have to tell them about my spiritual sacrifice? I would probably have to tell them, to keep them from worrying about me. And then if I had Abner with me, they would see what a sacrificial servant's heart I did have, and there I would be in the midst of my brothers and sisters, the fasting servant, admired for my spiritual maturity.

But on the other hand, would I go at all? Maybe I had outgrown them; they were a pretty religious bunch, tending toward legalism, and I didn't really want to wear a suit and tie anymore. I wanted to be more laid back, sort of in the California Vineyard style, though without the controversy. No, I wasn't much of a theologian; I simply wanted to be comfortable. Not complacent, of course, but comfortable in my faith, as long as it was orthodox, whatever that was; there seemed to be disagreement over that too.

Yes, Christians were strange. An odd bunch, really. All fighting over this, that, and the other thing. Just like ordinary people. I looked at the lump of poor Abner there. What did he believe? He said Christians were plastic, unreal hypocrites. That was easy to say, of course, and easier to prove. Oh well, what was I going to do with him? Mother wouldn't be pleased. Or would she? You could never figure Mother sometimes. She might feed him for a few days. He could have my food. Yes, I would then be sacrificing my food, so that someone else could eat in my place, and I would get the reward.

Man, was I ever getting sick of this whole fasting business. That's all I thought about. It was becoming boring too. I resolved to think less about it in the future. I would devote myself more to detective work and think less about food. Yes, Joe LaFlam was by profession a detective, a serious, hard-nosed detective, but with a compassionate Christian heart, a man with a mission to solve the crime, to right the wrongs, and to save the lost. I suddenly realized I had been thinking of myself in the third person. Was that a sign of objectification and fragmentation of the self? And what did that mean? I wondered what my inner child thought, but I hadn't been in touch with him since I was a little boy, so there wasn't much chance of getting an answer from him right now when I needed it; I would have to commit some time to him and do a little more digging to find out what he really thought, but not now. Man, was I getting hungry.

I beeped my cell on and poked the numbers of Mrs. Mulligan. The guy who answered was, I suspected, her bodyguard. Or was he?

"Mrs. Mulligan there?" I said.

"Who's calling?"

"Joe. Joe LaFlam, private detective."

"Oh, yes, I see . . . she's not in."

"Tell her I know the score."

"Tell her you know the score?"

"You got it."

"As you wish."

I beeped him off first, before he could beep me off. I wasn't to be messed with. I had a hunch, and I wanted to see just what response that little bit of information would get from Mrs. Mulligan.

My hand vibrated. Just as I thought. She was sniffing the bait. I beeped.

"Joe LaFlam," I said knowingly.

"What score, Mr. LaFlam?"

"Uh, you know . . . the score."

"No. I don't know. And unless you have some further information to tell me about my daughters, I expect you to meet me at your office at ten tomorrow. In the meantime I do hope you will be spending your time doing whatever it is you are supposed to do to see that my daughters are returned home, instead of wasting your time phoning here to give us your latest sports updates."

She beeped me. Hmm, I thoughtfully beeped her too. She was either a good actor or my hunch was wrong. Either way it looked like I was going to be making the ransom run again tomorrow. I hoped the rain would hold off another day. Looking over at my couch, I wondered what I was going to do with Abner. He would survive just as well sleeping there. Why move him? Mother wouldn't like the smell anyway. I'd leave him here until tomorrow. Yes, that was the best plan.

"Abner," I yelled, "I'm going out. If you get hungry . . . well, I don't know. Food isn't everything. I'll be back tomorrow."

"Stop yer yellin'," Abner moaned into the couch. "Can't ya see I'm concentratin' on stayin' alive. And don't go worryin' yerself about me, I'm full of deviled egg."

"Fine," I whispered.

"Fine, what's fine? There's nothin' I can think of that's fine. Why don't you go drum up an insurance fraud or somethin'?"

I left Abner to his misery and headed out to the street. I needed to clear my head. I decided to walk down the street as if I had no cares. Yes, careless in Seattle, my town. I was thankful the air was still dry today, not filled with rain the way the air usually was this time of year in the Pacific Northwest rain forest. The forest, of course, had long since been chopped away to clear a space for the city, but the rain and the threat of rain had remained. The lowering clouds stared down wistfully at my town, no doubt now missing the long-gone, lush treetops of green replaced by the concrete and glass stand-ins, symbols of human folly, sticking upward, grasping to conquer the gray, monotone sky.

Yes, my head was clearing out the rubbish, and my legs felt springy, not weak in the knees the way they had been off and on for the last few days. I was glad to be alive without a care in the world. Who said this kind of weather was depressing? Christians weren't supposed to be depressed anyway.

But what about those who were? And was Prozac a good thing? And just how many people in America were medicated so they could stay in the rat race? Wasn't it all a bit unnatural? Perhaps there was something wrong if Christians and non-Christians had to take equal amounts of antidepressants. What was wrong with us believers? The message of Jesus was certainly true. So that could only mean there was something the matter with us. Or maybe we hadn't heard the message correctly because our plump, American hearts were so full with the cares of acquiring.

Oh well, I wouldn't be solving all the dilemmas of our day in one afternoon. I had my own case to solve, one I was being paid for; at least I hoped I was going to be paid, and then I remembered I'd forgotten to tell Mrs. Mulligan that in addition to my ransom delivery fee, I also got $75 a day, plus expenses. The business end had never been my strong suit. I only hoped I would never get a visit from the IRS.

But what about the Mulligans? That was the question. I had to lay a snare for those fraudulent kidnappers. And what about their motive? I had to find out the score because Mrs. Mulligan didn't seem to know it. Maybe she was on the up-and-up. But why wouldn't she be? And if she was, why would she trust me? Why would any of them trust me? No, something was wrong here. I was being set up. Well, they wouldn't get away with it tomorrow. Not this time. No more taking my eyes off the ransom, and no more apple juice on the stakeout.

I resolved to go home and see my mother, confident that nothing she might say would upset me today. And Abner would be fine, and I would get a good night's sleep, and tomorrow this whole kidnapping scam would be history. I returned to the parking garage, climbed aboard my Mustang and gunned it for home.

The aroma saturated the house. My mother had cooked my favorite meal for dinner, shepherd's pie and peas, the way only she could make it. I did wonder why she had made my favorite meal when she knew I was fasting, but I knew discipline required that I accept her choice for dinner graciously without question and without suspicion of impure motives. I found her in the kitchen humming over her labor of love.

"Why are you making that when you know I'm not eating?"

"I enjoy it too, dear. You wouldn't want me to deny myself, would you? You're the one fasting, not me."

"Bless you," I said and then went upstairs to my room without further comment, my mother calling after me, "You could just sit with me, dear,"

I closed my door decisively.

# CHAPTER THIRTEEN

The next morning I found Abner asleep in the same position I'd left him. When I entered, he grumbled into the couch, "A few more hours to go." I opened the window. The room's fumes escaped outward and upward. I looked at the rain drizzling down. It had begun during the night; I hoped it would stop before Bertie's ransom delivery, although that wasn't essential. A little rain wouldn't hurt me. I was above petty trials now. My pace of life today had slowed to a rate where I knew I could peacefully assess every situation and endure every provocation. My character was being built on a firm foundation of sacrifice.

I had even seen a change in my countenance in the mirror this morning while shaving; I had perceived a brighter face shining back, whether the result of a cleansed system or of a spiritual awakening, or a combination of both, I did not know. All I knew was that today I was being carried along in a stream of peace. And I now knew why the saints of old were painted with halos.

"I suppose ya were up all night bakin' me a devil's food cake," Abner mumbled and then snickered to himself.

He couldn't upset me. I was too far above the common fray. I sincerely wondered if I was long for the detective business. At this rate of growth, by the end of twenty-one days, I would be raising the dead on a regular basis. My sleep had even been hiked up a notch. Most of the night I had been dreaming spiritual dreams about my coming Kingdom victories, and consequently I had overslept, leaving me once again with no time to pray. I expected that

Mrs. Mulligan would be arriving soon, and even though the whole kidnapping affair was becoming entirely too mundane, I still needed to solve the case. I couldn't leave the detective business, if indeed that's what God was calling me to do, with a dirty slate.

"Is that all ya do . . . just sit there?" Abner mumbled again.

The knock came and the door opened. Mrs. Mulligan's body-guard entered, carrying a suitcase, and then came Mrs. Mulligan, who was sporting a cane. She glared over at Abner, still in his fetal position, and sniffed the air.

"Your mentor?" she said.

I would not be baited. I was above her disdain. There was no doubt in my mind the poor woman was the victim of an evil spirit, although I had no desire to engage in the controversy over whether Christians could be demonized. I knew it was easy to say, "The devil made me do it," but, on the other hand, could the bad behavior of many Christians simply be attributed to weak will and undeveloped character? God only knew.

"Please have a seat," I said graciously, trying to imagine her as my mother-in-law. Her bodyguard gave me the once over, and, strangely, I thought I saw his eyes become misty, but it was probably just the fumes.

"It's cold in here," Mrs. Mulligan said, unamused.

"I'll close the window if you like."

"Yeah, close the window," Abner growled. "I'm freezin'."

"No, that's fine," Mrs. Mulligan said. "That would only concentrate the smell, and, besides, we only intend to be here a minute. Here is the money."

Mrs. Mulligan pointed her cane at the suitcase, which her man then placed on my desk. He popped it open. There were a lot of dreams in there, but I was above such carnal lusts now. I was living in the spiritual realm, soaring free of earthly constraints. The lure of riches no longer had a hold on me, those fickle riches that promised the world to those who would serve the god of mammon.

No, I was now liberated from the temptation these big bills offered, sharp and clean as they were, and crisp and green, lined up neatly and compactly, secure in their case, one million beautiful dollars, holding the promise of condos on every continent, Corvettes and Lincolns and wom—.

"You're drooling, Mr. LaFlam," Mrs. Mulligan said. "Would you like to count it?"

"Oh, sorry," I said. "I've got this excess saliva with nothing to do. I haven't been eating lately."

"Neither have I," Abner yelled.

"Don't worry, Mrs. Mulligan," I said confidently. "I'll deliver the ransom, and your daughters will be home shortly, or my name isn't Joe LaFlam."

Not enthused by my assurance, Mrs. Mulligan rose to go.

"See you do it right, Mr. LaFlam."

"I will, Mrs. Mulligan. Now would you like to settle our account today?"

"I think a more appropriate time would be when the job is done, don't you think, given the circumstances and your success to date?"

I remembered I was above all this and said, "Of course, Mrs. Mulligan, I do see your point. But . . . uh . . . I did forget to tell you I also charge seventy-five a day plus expenses."

"How unfortunate you didn't mention it before, and, Mr. LaFlam?"

"Yes, Mrs. Mulligan?"

"You might want to do something about your breath."

The bodyguard opened the door. Mrs. Mulligan glanced over her shoulder at the back of reclining Abner and then exited, her nose elevated, followed by her man. I sat reflecting. I was above all this.

"Yer sure a smooth talker," Abner said. "No wonder ya have to drive a cab." He rolled onto his back and added, "Let me get this straight. Ya sit drivin' a cab all night so ya can rent this place to sit in all day."

I would not be provoked. He rolled back on his side and snorted a laugh into the couch. He said, "At that rate you'll end up sleepin' under cardboard in an alley."

"I'm glad you're feeling better," I said, proud of my self-control in the face of being confronted with my fear of being left destitute, a useless nobody, foraging for scraps in the damp, trickling alleys of civilization gone wrong. But those kinds of thoughts were far from me now. In the process of cutting my ties with daily bread, I had also been released from the fear of death, even from the fear of dying badly. After all, what did it matter, as long as I was doing God's will?

"Why don't ya get a real job?" Abner grumbled.

I looked at the suitcase again. It seemed a real shame to dump this million into the trash can, but that's what I was getting paid for, if and when I finally did get paid. I wondered why I should bother staking out the can at all. I had even lost my desire to chase down my own $20,000. Why not just chuck the million in and leave. That's all I was getting paid for, if and when I got paid. What was a million here or there in this game? I suspected it was all going to the same cause anyway, except, of course, for the $200,000 that had gone to my Spelunker conspirator friend. I wondered why he hadn't tried to kill me lately. I hoped he wasn't ill again.

Yes, I would drop the money off and leave. It was simply not my responsibility after that. And forget my $20,000. I'd get some of it back in fees, eventually, I hoped. The way I figured it now, either Canute would let Brittany and Bertie go and would keep the money, or Canute and Brittany would let Brittany and Bertie go, and Canute and Brittany would keep the money, or Canute and Brittany and Bertie would let Brittany and Bertie go, and they would all keep the money. In the first case, Brittany and Bertie were the victims; in the second, Bertie was the victim; and in the third, Mrs. Mulligan was the victim. Then again, in the first case, if Canute was the sole culprit, he might murder Brittany and Bertie and make off with the money. But I reassured myself again that none of my clients ever got killed in my cases.

So who was really doing what to whom and for what reason? If Canute was the lone kidnapper, then he profited big time. If Brittany was in on it with Canute, then how did Brittany benefit when it was all family money? And if Brittany and Bertie were in on it with Canute, then how could they possibly benefit when, again, it was their money in the first place? And, another question, who was this King Canute anyway?

"Ya do just sit there all day long, don't ya?" Abner said.

"I've got a delivery to make," I said unperturbed. "I'll be back in a few hours."

"Sure, and do hurry. Yer favorite chair'll be waitin' for ya, sittin' there all alone, gettin' cold."

# CHAPTER FOURTEEN

Through the drizzled windshield I eyed the park, the monkey cage, the trash can, and then I looked down at the suitcase beside me. There was a lot of cool green in there. What was stopping me from just driving away with it? No, I couldn't do that simply because I wasn't absolutely positive none of my clients ever got killed in my cases. How could I take the chance on Brittany and Bertie buying the farm? I was a Christian. I had to make the drop. I was only a pawn in their game. Who wanted to be a millionaire anyway?

I grabbed the suitcase and got out of the car. I walked across the mushy grass toward the now-familiar trash can, trying to remember if they were called trash cans in America, and remembering that in Canada, where I lived long ago, a place I hardly thought about anymore, they were called garbage cans. I reached my goal and realized the suitcase wasn't going to fit. They should really have foreseen this. What was I supposed to do now? The rain began to pound down in big dollops. Then I remembered. The top on these things came off. I removed the lid, crammed the suitcase into the garbage can and then replaced the lid. Yes, that's what they paid me for, fast thinking on the job. I gave a superior nod to the monkeys in the cage and then retraced my mushy way back across the grass, the rain plopping down.

Back inside my Mustang, I felt safe from the rain. I turned on the engine and cranked the heater on high. I would dry in no time, and today I would keep my eyes peeled. I had already made up my mind. They weren't going to get away with the money on my shift again. Sure, I could drive away, and sure, I'd given the idea some serious thought, but if I did drive away, then I wouldn't be a detective anymore. No, if I decided to do that, I would be a different man with a different destiny. I would no longer be me; I'd be somebody else. Somebody else, living a different life; I would not know me anymore. Who would I then be? God only would know.

But the fact was that I wasn't going to just drive away, so I would stay being me; I wouldn't have to be somebody else who only then would look like me but wouldn't be the essence of me anymore. Choices. We all had choices, and I chose to stay me, the way I was, a detective, and a darn good one at that, despite what I sometimes thought about me and my abilities.

I thought I saw the can move. There was nobody around but . . . there! The can did it again. There was no wind and yet the can jiggled. I definitely smelled a rat this time. I sprang from my Mustang and sprinted through the mushy grass toward the trash can. Once there I ripped off the lid. Sure enough, the can was empty. I tipped and rolled it. A false bottom. Underneath, a manhole cover clinked into place. The kidnapper was no more than a few feet away, underground, with nothing between us except for this thick, iron cover that wouldn't budge. I couldn't pry it up. They had secured it somehow from underneath. I was beaten.

"You won't get away with this," I yelled at the manhole.

"You were only supposed to deliver the ransom," a muffled male voice said from below. "Can't you read a ransom note? Now I'll have to kill somebody."

"You won't kill anybody!" I yelled, irritated. "Nobody ever gets killed in my cases, and I'm pretty sure about that, Mr. King Canute."

"Sure, sure, LaFlam. And while I've got you, what happened to the last $200,000? Did you lose it?"

"Spelunkers."

"Spelunkers?"

"Yeah, and come to think of it . . ."

"Got to go. Keep up the good work."

"Wait a minute, Canute, I've got a question for you. Canute? King?"

It was no good. He'd kept his word. He was gone. I tried to remove the cover again. No use. I wondered where the sewer came out, but by the time I would discover the answer to that question Canute would be long gone. I looked up and realized I now had another challenge to face. The police cruiser had arrived.

"Get in, LaFlam," the officer said.

# CHAPTER FIFTEEN

When I got back to the office, Abner was still in a fetal position. He grumbled something in his sleep about Tequila Sunrise. I sat in my chair, read some more of *The Fast Life*, and waited for her. It didn't take long. The door opened and there she stood. The best of the bunch. Penelope, in all her youthful splendor. About twenty-one or -two, I guessed, athletic, nubile, and voluptuous with Cleopatra-black hair. Would I ever marry? Her? I didn't have a chance.

"Joe LaFlam?" she said. Her voice was sweet, not sickeningly sweet like cotton candy but perfectly sweet like Mom's apple pie with just the right amount of cinnamon, and the crust flaky, not heavy, and on top, a scoop of vanilla ice cream to make my day.

"In the flesh," I said enthusiastically. "Have a chair. I suppose you've come about your mother. Kidnapped, no doubt. Never mind the note. Will I deliver the ransom? Of course. Two million, you say. Noon tomorrow. Oh, that King Canute. Into the trash can . . . and, of course, I know you can't pay me now . . . but that's OK."

"How . . . how could you know all that? The ransom note just came to the house . . . except there's nothing about a trash can."

"What? No trash can? Let me see that note."

Sure enough, Canute had changed the drop zone. He wanted the money left at the train station. Of course, he knew I wasn't going to fall for the false-bottom trash can routine again. No, I was wise to that old caper. He knew he wasn't dealing with some rank amateur. And they'd given us till Monday? But of course, the banks were closed Sunday. I got a day off.

"See?" she said. "They'll kill her if we don't do as they say. And my sisters . . . too . . . they haven't—"

"Don't worry, none of my clients ever get killed in my cases. And by the way, what happened to your mother's bodyguard? Is he missing too?"

"Bodyguard? Oh, sure . . . no, I don't know . . . I haven't seen him since . . . I'm not sure."

"Never mind then. Have you got the full two million?"

"I can get it."

"You can get it without your mother's signature?"

"Our lawyer can get it, and, besides, I'm the major shareholder in our family. Daddy and Mother . . . well, you see . . . and my sisters . . . well, they . . . I don't know . . . that's the way it worked out in my dad's will."

Well, well, well. Motive. I finally had the motive. They were all conspiring to bilk darling Pen because she had been the favourite, or favorite here in America. How could I possibly break the news to her?

"Your mother and sisters are felons," I said.

"What do you mean? They've been kidnapped. They could be killed. They're not criminals; they're victims."

"Kill the witches," Abner growled in his sleep.

"Who's he?" darling Pen said.

"Some of my street ministry," I said.

"Bless you," she said.

I suddenly *was* feeling blessed; the case was practically solved; nobody was going to get killed, and I was in the company of beautiful Pen. I started to think about my fast, but then remembered I wasn't going to think much about that anymore, so instead I took my chair for a spin and shot three, lightning-quick poofs in. Darling Pen's mouth fell open.

"It's OK; it helps me to think."

"I see, but do you think—"

"No problem. Bring the money Monday and you can come with me to make the drop. I'll take good care of you. Is that OK?"

"I think so. I don't really have anyone else to ask."

"Don't worry; you'll have them back soon. I guarantee the kidnappers will let them go. And they'll all be richer for it too."

"Richer?"

"Never mind, you'll soon see, or my name isn't John Doe."

"But your name isn't."

"It's OK; I'll explain soon . . ."

"And I'm Abner Doubleday," Abner exclaimed from the couch.

"Can I give you a ride home?" I asked Pen.

"No, I have my own car but thanks."

"Monday morning then, and don't worry. I have the key to setting them free. Your loved ones will be home safe and sound, I guarantee. And come to think of it, I'll pick you up at your bank. You can't be carrying that amount of money around by yourself."

"Fine," she said. "The Royal Bank on Granville."

"Good, Washington Mutual on Third."

"Huh? No, the Royal—."

"Good, eleven Monday then."

She rose to leave. I, the gentleman, stood. She offered me her hand. I took it gratefully.

"You're sure they'll let them go?" she said, withdrawing.

"Indeed," I replied, loosening my grip.

"Ya can forget it," Abner said. "He just sits there all day."

"Hallucinating," I said.

"Yes, I see," she said, and then turned and glided gently out of my office.

"Ya got any grub in this place?" Abner said, sitting up on the couch, still clutching himself, his eyes beginning to clear.

　　"No, but you can come home with me if you want. My mother will probably feed us."

　　"Ya live with yer mother?"

# CHAPTER SIXTEEN

Mother wasn't pleased initially. She twitched her nose a few times at first sight but then settled into a homey acquiescence and a self-assurance that had come with age. She had never been a fearful woman, the worst having happened years before with the death of my father. I had never known him, and Mother hadn't kept any pictures of him either, which I always thought strange. I was never able to find out much about him from Mother either. It was always too painful for her to discuss, and for that reason I had never pressed her on the issue.

"So your name's Abner," Mother said as we sat in the living room getting acquainted.

"Right," I said. "He's a member of our church. You must have seen him there." I suspected she hadn't because she wasn't dedicated to regular attendance, preferring instead to stay home Sunday morning to watch television, and Abner hadn't been coming that long either.

"I can talk fer myself," Abner said.

"I knew an Abner years ago," she said wistfully.

"Ya, how long ago?" Abner said.

"More than thirty years now."

Abner slowly leaned forward to take a better look at Mother.

"Margaret . . . that you?"

"Abner? Oh, no . . . Abner?"

"Well, I'll be," Abner said, stunned.

They both sat staring at each other for the longest time, and then they shifted their gaze to me. What a coincidence—the two of them not seeing each other for more than thirty years and now here they were, sitting in the same living room together because I had found my mother's dear, old friend sleeping in an alley.

"We only knew each other a brief time," Mother said to me. "I wasn't a Christian then."

"I sure wasn't," Abner said, "and I'm not altogether convinced I'm one now. Comes and goes."

"Would you excuse us, dear," my mother said. "I think we would like to get caught up, and you won't be eating dinner anyway."

"Yes, I would like some time alone," I said, cooperating with Mother. "I'll go up to my room for a quiet time. What's the use of fasting if you don't do any praying?"

I laughed alone at my inside joke.

"I haven't eaten since yesterday," Abner said, looking at me accusingly.

Ignoring his shot, I said to Mother, "I'm sure you'll be safe here with Abner."

I laughed again, good-naturedly, and left the room.

I sat on my bed, propped up on my pillows, deep in thought. Was it possible? Incredible as it was. But no doubt I would soon find out the whole story. Life, I knew, was filled with surprises, twists, and turns, but this? Had Penelope truly been victimized by her own family? Probably. There was a whole lot of money at stake, and when money was involved, anything could happen.

Yes, there was a lot to think about. I sneaked a thought about fasting too. My thought was how well I felt and how I might seemingly go on fasting forever. And then I stopped thinking about it, as I had earlier promised.

So Mother and Abner knew each other. Small world. I wondered if he had been a friend of my father's, and if he had known him, maybe he would tell me more about him—who he was, what he did, how he died. One would have thought that I, being a detective and all, might have found those important details out by now. But no, there was always something that held me back. Did I really want to know? Sometimes I had feared the worst, that Mother had been hiding something from me, that I didn't know the whole truth. But why would my mother lie to me?

No, I had to think happier thoughts. Penelope. Man, maybe I would marry after all. But was I too old for her? No, a dozen or so years didn't make any difference. Yes, twelve years would be perfect. I would be just mature enough to be in charge. Of course I knew women wouldn't stand for the domineering type these days, but at least I would have a head start in having my emotional needs met.

And she was an heiress. What a twist of fate—although I didn't believe in fate—that would be. I truly would be blessed then, and, no, it certainly wouldn't be fate at all but the righ-teous result of the proper application of Christian principles. I sow a twenty-one-day fast and reap an heiress, a beautiful, young one. But what about love? Oh, that would grow to full bloom in the warm earth of affluence. And we could pick and choose where we wanted to minister, if indeed we did decide to enter the mission field. But, then again, perhaps supporting missions financially was the ideal thing, and then we could dedicate our lives to building up the local church, using our money and influence to see that the building of God's kingdom was done correctly.

I examined my recent thoughts and wondered how they could have materialized in a fasted mind. Without a doubt, the flesh was strong. And was I truly growing in the faith? I decided to pray. But, no . . . I remembered suddenly; I had to drive the cab tonight, and I only had twenty minutes to get there. No time to pray. I dashed for the kitchen and a glass of Clamato.

"You'll just make it," Mother said, hesitating between bites.

"Cab driver by night, private eye by day," Abner said. "Yer gonna end up sleepin' in an alley."

Ignoring Abner's assessment, I gulped the clammy juice.

"Now, Abner," Mother said.

"Unbelievable," he added.

# CHAPTER SEVENTEEN

It was a slow cab night in the rain. I thought about Brittany; I thought about Bertie; I thought about Penelope. I thought about life. I thought about my leaving Mother there with Abner. Was that a good idea? Still, Mother hadn't seemed to mind. And what was my responsibility? None. She was the mother; I was the son. It was her house; end of story.

On to better thoughts. Penelope. Hmm, Pen. Elope with Pen. What a thought. Envelope Penelope. Hmm, synapses misfiring. Syn. Synergy. Christians coming together would no doubt create synlessergy. Slow night all right. I opened my pocket Bible, looking for a sign. It opened to Romans 8:1. "There is therefore now no condemnation to those who are in Christ Jesus, who do not walk according to the flesh, but according to the Spirit." So, I wasn't condemned. I was walking in the Spirit. There was hardly anything you could think of to do that was much more spiritual than fasting. Of course there was martyrdom, and there was celibacy, but I had a good hunch—though, of course, I didn't make decisions based on hunches—I would be spared those sacrifices.

Yes, I was content. I was indeed walking in the Spirit. I closed my Bible, knowing the next few verses were a little harder to understand. I meditated briefly on being free of condemnation. Then I opened my pocket Bible again.

This time it opened to John 3:16. I knew it—another sign. I would soon lead someone to the Lord. I had never done that before. "For God so loved the world that He gave His only begotten Son, that whoever believes in Him should not perish but have everlasting life." Simple. Everyone could understand that. So why didn't they? Hmm. Moving on to John 3:19–21: "And this is the condemnation, that the light has come into the world, and men loved darkness rather than light, because their deeds were evil. For everyone practicing evil hates the light and does not come to the light, lest his deeds should be exposed. But he who does the truth comes to the light, that his deeds may be clearly seen, that they have been done in God." Never saw that before. There was that word *condemnation* again. Heavy word. But why didn't people get the message? Why didn't I get it sometimes? Serious questions.

Not wanting to get bogged down, I closed my pocket Bible and got my Christian novel out from under the seat. I opened at my gold-tasseled bookmark. I was about halfway through. The story was about the Antichrist and some folks being raptured, and the rest of the folks are left here on the planet to figure it out. I then wondered if Christians should write fiction. As Christians we were supposed to be representing the truth and presenting the facts, not making stuff up.

But then again, Jesus told stories. But His stories had a real point to them. Yes, there was no question that God's stories were better than the ones we on earth made up. But God created us so we could create, too, so maybe it was all right to make up a few stories. But what happens when God's story gets mixed up with our stories? Maybe it was OK to tell stories if our stories somehow told about His story. Of course His story had the eternally happy ending, and there was no doubt that everyone's life had to have an ending, and a beginning, and, most of the time, a middle. And all we had to do was introduce His story into ours to have a happy ending. And we could mix both stories together, as long as we presented His accurately.

Yes, that was probably OK; I had some peace about it. We only needed to tell our stories truthfully, the best we could, when we mixed them with His. I opened my novel to where I left off and wondered if I would be raptured tonight.

Outside the water poured down. I looked up to see a man peering in my passenger window, a strangely familiar man. He was pointing a gun. I had a choice. I could roll the dice—although, of course, I never played craps—and speed away or await my fate, though, as I said, I didn't believe in fate. Unfortunately, although I didn't believe in fortune either, my cab wasn't running. I was saving gas. In the short time it took for me not to make a hasty decision (although there was none really to make because trying to start the engine would delay my "speeding away" option by several crucial seconds), the man opened the passenger door and entered gun first.

"Well, smart guy, enjoying your reading?" he said, closing the door. "Nice title. Don't worry. You won't be left behind; you'll be going first."

The Small Man laughed softly.

"Where to?" I said.

"A smart guy to the end. Well, smart guy, let's take ourselves a little ride. Never mind the meter."

"Since I'm going to die, do you mind if I try to lead you to the Lord? I've never led anyone to the Lord, and that's the one thing I wanted to do before I died. I know the chances are slim, but still I'd like to try because I've been fasting faithfully. I had wanted to get married, too, but there's no time for any of that now, especially since I am fasting."

"Are you finished?"

"The wages of sin is death."

"Well, smart guy, you're about to be paid off in full."

"What if you were to die today, this very night, you know, with your heart in the condition it's in, do you know where you will be spending eternity?"

"Not with you."

"There's only one hope for you in this world, and that's to give your life to Jesus Christ."

"If I give my life to Him after I kill you, will that still count, smart guy?"

"Sure."

"Well, then I'll think about it after you're gone."

"I have to warn you, however, about one thing."

"What's that, smart guy?"

"Nobody ever gets killed in my cases."

"Not if you don't live to finish it, smart guy."

"Hmm."

"Turn left here."

"Say, look," I said, trying to be helpful, "I think someone's following us. They've been there for a few blocks now."

"What do you mean? Don't get smart, smart guy. Wait . . . I see. Turn at the next corner."

"See, the car's still following us."

The Small Man turned and nodded. "OK, step on it."

I gave it some gas to humor him and asked, "Were you brought up in a Christian home?"

"Catholic . . . and turn left here. It's no good; they're still there. But they're not the cops; they've got a Porsche."

"When's the last time you went to confession?"

"Uh, not since I was a kid. Who are those guys? You got any friends? Sorry, stupid question."

"So, you're a lapsed Catholic."

"Yeah, lapsed . . . I'm going to hell. Are you satisfied? There . . . head for the freeway, the on-ramp . . . good."

"No, I'm not satisfied. Kind of you to ask, though. I would be satisfied, I think, if I had a wife, kids, and a steady income. And, naturally, I'd want a good church home. One that is mature and not filled with all the problems you get when you have a lot of immature, dissatisfied people who are only out for themselves and not loving one another. But enough of me. Have you ever wanted to meet Jesus?"

"If you lose them, smart guy, I'll let you introduce me. Floor it!"

I floored it. I glanced at the conspirator. The oncoming headlights flashed on his face. The sweat on his brow glistened. Could his heart take it? Would his heart stop before it was reborn? In this life, that was the question we all had to answer.

The speedometer nudged up to ninety. In my rearview I saw the pursuing Porsche. The vanity plate read "CANUTE." But why? And why hadn't the Feds tracked him down? How many cars were named Canute? Nothing made sense as I sped down the highway of life. Death sat next to me, King Canute on my tail. Why? I asked. Why? No answer came. Then in a split second I heard it. It was a clang. A rod in the engine had pushed its last piston. The cab roared and sputtered. Black smoke blasted out the back. We jerked, limping to the side of the road. I brought my dead cab to a halt. Car 66 was done. From the seat beside me no sound came.

And then, "You . . . you . . . smart guy. Call me an ambulance."

The Small Man was in distress. His gun lay lifeless at his side. He crossed himself. The Canute Porsche had pulled over behind me. The showdown was now. I opened my door and climbed out.

"Call . . . me . . . one . . . now," the Small Man said.

I stared at the Porsche lights. Canute had to be in there. I strode toward my destiny. The Porsche's engine revved; the rear wheels spat gravel. It lunged and then paused as it passed by. The dark-tinted passenger window descended a crack.

"So, you're all right," the Canute voice said, the same one I heard speak from under the manhole cover. "Make sure the ransom gets there, see."

He revved some more and dropped the clutch. Gravel sprayed. The Canute Porsche screamed down the highway in the rain. I resolved from now on to pack my piece at all times. Then I remembered the Small Man's gun. But it was too late. Back inside my cab he was sweating. I took the mike and his gun.

"Sixty-six."

"Go, 66."

"This cab's dead on the I-5, just past Bothell."

"How'd you get there, 66?"

"Gimme the mike," the Small Man said.

"Are you sure you have the strength?" I asked, concerned, handing him the mike.

"Send . . . an ambulance . . . Highway 1, just past the tunnel. Hurry."

# CHAPTER EIGHTEEN

It was Sunday. I had a day's grace from ransom delivering. I took Abner to the 10:00 A.M. service. He had been strangely silent all morning, no doubt under conviction for his backsliding. Mother had opted, as usual, to stay at home with the television.

We entered the sanctuary, breezing passed the greeters. Melinda Swartz saw me coming and turned around in her seat. Melinda was desperate to find a man. She was a young, attractive woman, but she had a handicap: she was manipulating, controlling, and intimidating. Tempting all right, but I wasn't stupid.

"Your mother not feeding you properly?" Melinda said as we passed by.

I smiled kindly. Her insinuation that I was too old to be living at home fell to the ground, and I was seasoned enough now not to retaliate by telling her about my twenty-one-day, juice-only fast. Yes, I had grown too much to fall for that one. Pride was no longer an issue.

Besides, I had almost made up my mind. I might just leave this church for good. Who needed to associate any longer with these insensitive people? Not me. Nobody seemed to notice my new spiritual glow either, and if they did notice they were probably too proud to mention it. How at any time could I have possibly felt a part of this congregation? No matter, I was on a higher level now. In that insightful moment I realized that spiritually, in one short week, my fast had matured me substantially.

We found two seats in my section, the one I always sat in, on the right side halfway up. That's where I had felt most comfortable the last eleven years, but not now. The days of the comfortable pew were over for me, although they weren't pews, they were metal chairs, double-stuffed to meet the needs of the affluent congregation.

Abner in his torn-jeans outfit stuck out like a sore bum in the rich sanctuary with everyone dressed in their Sunday garb, worshiping the god of mammon. Not me anymore. I was committed now to the church of the street.

Pen and I, if, indeed, Pen and I did become "us," would use our money to feed the poor. Unless, of course, Brittany was innocent, and then maybe she was the one, but there was little hope of that, and then there was Bertie, and she, too, might be innocent. And then there was Mrs. Mulligan, but, naturally enough, she didn't figure into that equation, and then again we came back to dearest Pen. She was the most likely bet, although, of course, I didn't gamble. But who really knew which one was for me? And was I fickle?

"I'm not comin' here again," Abner grumbled. "They're pretendin' not to stare."

"Well, if you're not, neither am I," I said with conviction.

We all stood for the first song. The lyrics were from an old hymn, but the tune had been hopped up a bit for current consumption. The idea was to be a church of inclusion. Leadership didn't want to alienate the older ones, hence the lyrics, but they also wanted to appeal to the younger ones, hence the lively rendition. And they felt strongly that God wanted it that way, too, because they were positive God wouldn't want them to fight. I sang out unashamed; Abner hummed his way through.

After the worship we sat down and had a time of prayer for those whom God had put on people's hearts. People called out names. I wasn't sure if I should but then decided God would know who I meant.

"The Small Man," I intoned in turn.

Hardly anyone stared at me. Abner mumbled something about private eyes. As other names were spoken I zoned out, reflecting on the Small Man's chances for survival on the planet. The intern at the emergency ward had recognized him from his previous visits there. I had felt led this time to go with him to the hospital to continue on with my witness, not wanting him to depart from this existence with no hope. He had been too weak to object. It had been another heart attack all right, and they admitted him for treatment.

Realizing I wasn't much comfort to him despite my best intentions, I left him there with my promise to return. His last words to me were spoken softly as I left. "Nice taxi, smart guy." In return I good-naturedly said, "I know you're a Spelunker, but remember, you don't want to be going underground quite yet." He only groaned.

I sat politely through the sermon. Pastor Bob's message was on humility: God resists the proud but gives grace to the humble. I could identify. After he was through, we sang another song, and then I headed for the door and freedom without further comment to anyone. I knew I would seriously have to consider whether I would ever return. And if I did decide to leave, I would go and talk to the pastor about my decision face-to-face. Not like some others who just disappeared without having the courage to confront their former shepherd. I'd heard that some now took advantage of the Internet and e-mailed their desertion. And I also knew that most people, when they first joined a church, took a lot of time cultivating a relationship with the pastor and the leadership, no doubt so they might be placed in the most favorable position to exhibit their best gifts for the benefit of all. But when they left they now could simply whip off an e-mail.

I, of course, wouldn't announce my intentions in such a cowardly way. But before I talked to Pastor Bob, maybe I would attend the First Church of the Manifest Presence a few Sundays to see if that might be the place for me. My decision would also hinge on the preference of the future Mrs. LaFlam. I resolved not to be heavy-handed. My wife deserved to have input too. Brittany, Bertie, Pen, whoever—she deserved to be heard.

"Yer mother said I could come back fer lunch," Abner said, catching up to me.

We climbed into my Mustang, and I wondered whether this would be a good time to visit the Small Man in the hospital.

"Well?" Abner said.

"Well what?"

"Lunch?"

"You know I'm not eat— Uh . . . oh, sure, you need food. I'll drop you off at home. I've got a mission."

"Yer on a mission all right."

"I've been meaning to ask if you knew my dad at all. You know, since you knew my mother back then."

"Yer dad? What was his name?"

"Allan. I think they called him Al."

"Uh . . . what happened to him?"

"Killed. I don't know all the details. Mother never liked to share."

"Sorry," Abner said and seemed to mean it.

"I'll drop you off," I said, wondering who Abner really was inside there.

# CHAPTER NINETEEN

I decided to go in for a minute with Abner to see if Mother was all right with my leaving them alone for lunch. After all, I wasn't eating anyway. She was more than happy with that. Mothers could be odd at times. I left them sitting quite happily at the kitchen table.

Back in my Mustang I drove in the direction of the hospital, contemplating my possible church move. Leaving was all tied in with the outcome of the case. So I would wait until then to make my decision. Patience was a fruit of the Spirit. Long-suffering was the less-desirable, King James translation. And I had indeed suffered, long and hard, waiting for the right mate. And I would continue to do so for as long as it took.

I felt at loose ends without a ransom to deliver, and Monday, though only the next day, seemed eternally far. I had time on my hands. Until you tried fasting you weren't aware of how much time was taken up eating every day, or anticipating eating or getting ready to eat or making the meal or going to where the food was. When you were fasting you had to do something with that extra time and, naturally enough, *The Fast Life* said you were supposed to use that time to pray. But praying was hard to do.

I pulled into the hospital parking lot, took my ticket, and slotted my car. I decided to pray before I went in to see the Small Man. But first I needed to catch up on the news. I had to stay in touch with the world, even though the newspeople didn't know what I knew about the grand scheme of things. I turned on the car radio and sat there with my engine running. It wasn't news time yet. A woman was calling into a talk show saying the Internet was a blight on the world. The host agreed and took another call, and I, knowing I was procrastinating, turned the radio off. It was then I had a revelation.

It was one of those pictures in my mind. I could see planet earth enveloped in spider webs. Yes, I suddenly could see it all plainly. The Internet was the devil's counterfeit for the Body of Christ. The devil was webbing the world with instant communication, an electronic organism that would suffocate the globe with the mediocrity of the alienated masses, the connections impersonal, the content being the banal lives of postmodern humanity. I had seen the Enemy's plan, and it was us. But God had a much better plan, the original plan. The Body of Christ was going to function as one with Jesus at the head. The communication would be spiritual and instant; who needed a modem for that? The enemy wasn't going to win with his silly Internet impersonation of the real thing.

Still, Christians could legitimately take advantage of the Internet until the real thing was perfected. But how long would that take? How long before the Body of Christ would mature? How long until all Christians on earth were simultaneously listening and obeying His commands? Or were we all going to be raptured first and only begin to pay attention in heaven? These were hard questions. Reflecting on my thoughts, I concluded that I should have stayed in college. A mind like mine was too precious to waste.

Inside the hospital I inquired at the reception desk and discovered the Small Man had been admitted and was scheduled to undergo a quadruple bypass. I found him on the second floor in ill humor.

"Where's my gun this time, smart guy?" he said. "Back in your safe? It would sure come in handy right about now."

"Don't stress yourself," I said. "You'll get it back when you're in good enough shape to use it. Loud noises aren't good for you right now."

"You ever heard of a silencer, smart guy?"

I ignored his nastiness and said, "I've been fasting for about a week now, and I was just wondering if you would mind if I prayed for you . . . you know, that God would heal you?"

"Then can I shoot you?"

"Sure, if that's what you have to do. As a Christian, it's only my job to pray for you."

"Yeah, OK, you pray for me, smart guy. What could it hurt? But no funny business."

I advanced toward the Small Man's bed and placed my hand on his shoulder. He looked at me suspiciously, and then for some reason closed his eyes. I was in a predicament now. I had been brave enough to ask, and now I had to come up with a prayer. I realized I had never really done this before, my desire to pray for him arising, no doubt, from altered brain chemistry.

"Well, smart guy, are you finished? I didn't hear anything, or are you only allowed to talk to God privately?"

"No, just relax . . . I haven't started yet." I summoned some courage and remembered what Jesus said in the Gospels when He healed people. "Be healed," I said, and then remembered, "in the name of Jesus." I waited.

"That's it?" he said, opening his eyes.

"Yeah, that's all I know."

"Impressive, smart guy."

"How do you feel now?"

"What do you mean how . . . hmm . . . hold on . . . I do feel strangely better, and I'm feeling a hot sensation flowing through my body, especially in my chest."

"Probably the effects of the medication."

"Hey, just a second," the Small Man said. "I feel really good suddenly." He sat up and added, "I'm feeling full of energy."

My praying must have rattled him. I looked at the heart monitor machine. From what little I knew about vital signs, they seemed normal.

"Hey, look at the readings," he said. "They're normal."

"Machine must be broken," I said.

The Small Man pushed his buzzer, calling for the nurse.

"I haven't felt this good in years. Good praying, smart guy."

"I don't think you should excite yourself—"

The nurse entered the room, eyed me suspiciously, and then checked his vital signs.

"I'm healed," the Small Man said exuberantly. "Smart guy prayed for me. Unplug me. I'm healed and I'm getting out of here."

"Hold on," the nurse said. "You're not going anywhere." She studied the monitor again. "The signs do look good," she said, eyeing me again. I shrugged my shoulders innocently. "I'll see if I can get a hold of your doctor," she said. "Meanwhile, you stay put." She hurried out of the room.

"You healed me, boy," the Small Man said, swinging his legs over the side of the bed, his face smiling, the picture of health.

"I can't heal anyone," I said humbly. "Only Jesus can heal people."

"Then I can still kill you?" he said, looking even happier.

"Don't get your hopes up. You better wait to hear what the doctor has to say."

He began to sing and swing his legs. "I'm healed . . . I'm healed . . . Jesus healed me . . . now I can kill smart guy after all."

Even though he seemed quite deluded, I decided this was as good a time as any to try to lead him to the Lord.

"You know," I said, choosing my words carefully, "the healing of your physical body isn't as important as the healing of your relationship to God the Father."

"What do you mean?" he said, laughing. "Jesus just healed me. Our relationship seems fine to me."

"No, you don't get it . . . you have to say the prayer."

"What prayer?"

"Repenting of your sins and asking Him into your heart."

"What do you mean? He just healed my heart. He must already be in there."

"You don't know He just healed you."

"You don't believe me? Then why did you pray?"

"Oh, that's just what we do. Nobody ever gets healed."

"Well, smart guy, God fooled you this time. And as for repenting, I'll do that after I shoot you."

What a cruel joke. I had come to lead the Small Man to the Lord, and now he was healed through my careless prayer—well enough to send me into eternity.

"You know what?" he said. "I don't think I will kill you after all. I feel like a new man. You didn't hear it, did you?"

"Hear what?"

"The voice."

"No, what voice?"

"After you prayed for me, a voice said, 'You're My child. You belong to Me.' It was Jesus talking to me personally."

This was getting eerily supernatural. He believed he was healed, and now he thought God was talking to him. In my church this was heresy. However, I was happy to hear he might not kill me. I knew what I had to do next.

"Now you need to join a Bible-believing church," I said.

"Like yours? Where do you go?"

"Uh . . . I'm not sure."

"You're not sure where you go to church? Man, you're a smart guy all right."

The nurse blew through the door, rescuing me from further questioning.

"The doctor's coming," she said, eyeing me and then the heart monitor machine. "They're still normal," she said. "This can't be happening."

"Believe it, sister," the Small Man said.

I wondered where he had learned Christianese all of a sudden or whether it had just come naturally.

He said confidentially to the nurse, "I'm a new man, sister. Jesus loves me."

The nurse looked at me. I shrugged my shoulders to let her know it wasn't my fault. Why did she have to blame me? I hated persecution. Actually, I hated the thought of persecution, having never experienced the real thing; that is, having never done much to deserve any; that is, having never really done anything to deserve any. Unless you included those people who made fun of me because I was a Christian detective, but, of course, that really wasn't persecution, that was more because people had difficulty accepting novelty. Suddenly, in the spiritual light of my present fasted condition, I realized I had a terrible fear of man.

The doctor came through the door and said, "What's all this then?"

Why was he impersonating an English bobby? But then he was suspicious-looking anyway. He was thin, not skinny thin, but healthy thin—the kind of thin you found with those who ate healthy food and jogged and thought the right thoughts all the time and lived in a peaceful zone. On the other hand, maybe he was simply on self-prescribed diet pills and Prozac; either way, I resented his trim superiority. Examining my most recent thoughts, I appreciated the sharpened discernment the fasting discipline had loosed in my life. The good doctor started listening to the Small Man's heart with his stethoscope.

"Hmm," he said, listening to his chest, "sounds pretty good."

"What do you mean?" the Small Man said. "It sounds perfect. I've never felt better. Let me out of here. God's just cleaned out my arteries."

"Hmm," the doctor said again. He looked over at me. I shrugged my shoulders. "Are you related?" he said.

"No, uh . . . we're not," I said.

"Well, all the readings are normal," he said. "I don't know what to tell you. This doesn't happen."

"It did, and I'm fine . . . and I'm leaving," the Small Man said, "and unhook me. I've had a miracle."

"Well, under the circumstances," the doctor said, "if you insist, we can't keep you."

He nodded to the nurse, who began to disengage the Small Man from the medical machinery. It was then I was struck with a thought. It hit me gently.

To the doctor I said, "Do you think I could get some documentation of this case? You know, a letter stating the condition he was in, your diagnosis, the need for a quadruple bypass, and now, you know, he's suddenly healthy. I know I was the one who prayed for him, but I don't want it for me. Only God would get the glory. Then I could give a testimony at church . . . that is, if I go back to my church, although any church would do . . . of how God healed him through the laying on of my hands . . . God doing the healing, of course."

"You must be a Christian," the doctor said.

"Well, yes," I said, "and I wonder if you could answer a question. I mean, I know you're a busy man, but what do you think about fasting? I've been on a clear-fluid fast for about a week now and I'm thinking it had some effect on the healing result—obviously adding some oomph, if you see what I mean and—"

"I don't give casual opinions," the doctor said, rather rudely I thought, considering what had just occurred and who he was talking to. He was probably jealous and annoyed because the Small Man had been healed by my hands without the need for surgery, and the good doctor was now minus a quadruple bypass fee.

"I'm out of here," the Small Man said, jumping to get his clothes from the locker.

"You're sure about this?" the doctor said to the Small Man. "I do recommend we do a few tests first. It would only be proper procedure."

"No way, I'm healed and I know it," the Small Man said. "I don't have medical insurance, and I'm not wasting good money on tests, even though I'm not poor, right, smart guy?"

"It'll go on your government health care," the doctor said.

"Don't you know I'm an American?" the Small Man said.

The doctor looked at the nurse. "He's an American?"

"We're all Americans here," I said.

The doctor and the nurse stared at me.

"Yep, I'm out of here," the Small Man said, pulling his pants on, throwing off his hospital gown, and reaching for his shirt.

"We can't stop you," the doctor said. They stared at me again.

"Well, smart guy, let's blow this dump, and thanks, Dr. Hart, for everything."

With that he exited; I followed, amazed at his faith. The man who had tried to kill me because I knew too much was now a brother in the Kingdom, all thanks to the gift of healing my fast must have stirred up.

As we descended in the elevator, the Small Man said, "He just told me leaving the Spelunkers would be a good idea."

"God's talking to you?"

"Yeah, we've got a relationship now, but I'm not so sure about leaving the Spelunkers. Nobody gets out alive."

Seizing a teachable moment, I said, "Christianity is like that too. It'll cost you your life."

"It will? I thought I was saved."

"You are . . . but those who lose their lives will save them."

"Huh?"

"Christianity is sort of opposite to the world's way of thinking. You're saved now, but now your old self has to die, so your new self can live."

"So either way I'm dead."

"Yeah, you got it, but now you're guaranteed eternal life with God."

"Interesting. So why did God heal my heart if the Spelunkers are just going to kill me?"

"Well, the healing got you saved, no question about that, and that's the important thing. But another major reason for your healing, I think, is so God could encourage me and release me in this great healing gift, which no doubt will have incredible benefit for the Kingdom."

"It's all about you, isn't it, smart guy?"

Since he was still in a baby-Christian state, I decided his arrogant question didn't really deserve rebuke.

We left the hospital, heading for the parking lot. The Small Man said, "What am I going to do now?" That was a good question. What did a former Spelunker conspirator and hit man do when he got saved?

"Any family?" I said.

"No."

"You can come over to my house for a start," I said.

"Might as well," he said, as we got into my Mustang, "I don't know where else I can go."

"My mother will be glad to offer us advice," I said.

"You live with your mother? Come to think of it, that makes sense."

We drove. I and my first convert. I suppressed my elation. There was no question. Fasting did help keep the emotions in check. I decided I would have to disciple him. Who better? And now the gift of healing had been released through me. I was well on my way to a full-blown healing ministry. A television show perhaps. The private detective business would soon be a thing of the past. Sure, I would miss it, but one had to move on in life. God was leading now, but I first needed to fulfill my obligation to the Mulligans and, by the looks of things, get a wife to boot. Yes, good-bye, penury, so long, alley; if things kept on at this rate, I would have to challenge the Church's official position on sinless perfection.

# CHAPTER TWENTY

B ack at the house, Abner was snoring on the couch. I called for
Mother and said to the Small Man, "You know, I don't know
your name."

"Alfred . . . Alfred Hurst," he said.

I called for Mother again and offered Alfred a seat in an arm-
chair facing Abner. Mother entered, wiping her hands on her apron.
She stopped and gave Alfred the once-over.

"This one's better dressed," she said to me. Then, looking over
at the snoring Abner, she said, "Are you collecting male baby boomers, dear?"

"This is my mother, Margaret," I said. "This is Alfred Hurst,
Mother."

"Margaret?" Alfred said. "Is that you?"

"Alfred?" Mother Margaret said. "Well, I'll be."

They stared at one another for a few seconds and then looked
over at me.

"You know each other?" I said.

"Years ago," Mother said. "Years ago."

"Over thirty," Alfred said, his mouth sort of open.

"Of course, I wasn't a Christian then," Mother said hastily.

"Nor I," Alfred said, too dramatically, I thought. "In fact I only
met God today."

"I led him to the Lord," I said humbly.

"Good, dear," Mother said and then raised her eyebrows toward
the noisy Abner. "Remember Abner?" she said.

Alfred said, "You're kidding."

"No, John found him in an alley and brought him home."

"A real detective," Alfred said, and then eyeing me quizzically said, "John?"

I was tired now. Healing people was exhausting. Mother looked at me knowingly as only Mother could.

"Yes, Mother," I said, "I need some time alone. And I'm sure you need time to get caught up."

"Smart guy you got there," Alfred said to Mother, as I left the room.

In my room I dismissed the affairs of the afternoon and wondered if I should get serious about talking to God—He'd obviously heard my prayer and healed Alfred at my request. I wondered, too, what He might have to say to me. He was talking to Alfred already. A new brother and already hearing from the Lord. How did that work? He didn't know the four spiritual laws yet, and he hadn't even said the prayer asking Jesus to come into his heart. Go figure. God was truly spiritual.

Lying back on my bed, I decided there was no time like the present. "Dear Father. . . ." Yes, that was the problem right there. Who was my father? I swallowed my anger because there was no sense bringing all that up again. "Dear Jesus, I need a wife." Was that too self-serving? Yes, of course it was. No wonder I never prayed. "Oh, Lord, what will become of me?" No, that was more of the same. "Well, Lord, it's You and me." No, too cavalier. How about, "You know me, Lord, better than I know myself . . . so who am I?" Hmm, I wasn't likely to get an answer to that one. Let's see, "Oh, God, what actually is my calling, or do I have one?" No, too selfish again. I was getting nowhere. That was the problem with praying.

Still, the Bible did say you could ask for things. "Dear Lord, may I have a lot of money and a wife of your choosing?" No, too much like Aladdin's lamp. Was He listening to me at all? Why should He? The fast. Yeah, I did have some leverage there. "Jesus, I have been fasting diligently, and You know why. If my motivation at the beginning was bad, I'm sorry. But if I could have a wife all the same then . . ." No, you couldn't trick Him either.

There had to be a way where the onus was on Him instead of me. Aha. "Lord, what is it You want me to do?" That was the question. I would be totally unselfish and wait for Him to tell me what He wanted me to do. But how was I supposed to hear? I knew He spoke to people. He had been talking to Alfred. How did that work? I knew I would just have to wait. Oh well, I'd tried. "Dear Jesus, You know I tried, and I'm just waiting on You now." There, now I only had to wait to see what would happen next.

I would live my life the best I could while I was waiting for His answer. "And if my requests are OK with You, would You please grant them. And if You'll notice, I'm not being pushy either. I've learned that much. But I would almost certainly bring a lot of people into the Kingdom if You would only increase this healing gift. And, if I begin to empty hospitals, You will get all the glory. Amen."

There, I'd done it. I'd prayed. Now there were other matters to think about, not the least of which was what to do with Alfred. I was responsible for him now. But how did you disciple someone? Simple. I would by word and example teach him to be like me. He was older in age, but I was older in the Lord. And with any luck at all—though it went without saying I didn't believe in luck—he wouldn't despise my youth.

I felt some relief now that he wasn't out to kill me anymore. But was some other goon going to come after Alfred when the Spelunkers learned the score? And would I be the next one on their list? Yes, the danger wasn't altogether gone. But God would look after me, and He would take care of Alfred, too, for, of course, nobody ever got killed in my cases. I was a Christian detective and proud of it. And what God had me doing next, when He told me what He wanted me to do, I would be proud to do too. With that resolved, I took a well-deserved nap.

I awoke hearing loud voices from the living room. I had slept about an hour. I cleared my head by remembering what had happened earlier in the day. I looked at my healing hands. Where would it all lead? Then I remembered my nap dream. In it, I was in an alley at night under a dumpster, and three young women with flashlights were trying to get me to admit I was St. Paul, but I said, "That's impossible because I'm still looking for a wife." They seemed satisfied with that and left.

Then I was in the bathtub, playing with a rubber duck. My mother called and said my dad was on the phone. That's when I awoke, hearing loud voices coming from the living room. What might all that mean? Dream interpretation was hard. The loud voices came again. I went to investigate.

Abner was definitely awake when I entered the room. His face was red and solemn. Alfred in contrast had an ironical grin stuck to his face. Mother sat demurely in her chair.

"You had a rest, dear?" Mother said gently.

"What was all the noise about?" I said, not to be put off.

"Just a little disagreement," Mother said, "about the old days. Nothing really. We're all over it now."

"Yer over it," Abner said, "I'm . . ."

Mother raised one eyebrow. Abner shut his mouth. Boomers. They were a strange bunch.

"Ironic," Alfred said to me. "If I had done my job properly the first time, I wouldn't have met Jesus and I wouldn't be here now seeing your mother again."

"And I wouldn't have been released in my healing ministry," I said.

"And I wouldn't now be nearly ready to throw up," Abner said.

"Don't be testy," Mother said to Abner.

"Yeah, we're all one big happy Christian family now," Abner growled.

"Yes, we're all brothers and sisters in the Lord," I said, "except for me and Mother, who are, of course, mother and son."

"At least we're sure o' that," Abner mumbled.

Mother said sternly to Abner, "I don't want to have to ask you to leave."

So there we sat. Abner and Alfred had no place to go. They couldn't stay here with Mother and me, that was for sure. Abner was broke and homeless, and Alfred was on the run from the Spelunkers. One was a recovering backslider, the other a new believer. I needed to come up with a strategy fast.

Alfred, at least, had money. There was the $200,000 he had robbed from my safe, which had belonged to Mrs. Mulligan or, more precisely, to darling Penelope, or if it had gone to where it was supposed to go, then King Canute would have gotten it, along with Brittany or along with Brittany and Bertie or along with Brittany, Bertie, and Mother Mulligan, the latter seeming the most likely, the lot of them bilking sweet Penelope.

And what was Alfred's responsibility now as a Christian—to give the money back? But if he did, where did it rightly belong? If he had not interfered, the kidnappers had been scheduled to get it, or, at least, that had been Bertie's and Mrs. Mulligan's intention. But if they all were in on the caper, then the money rightly had to be returned to sweet Penelope because nobody was going to be killed if it wasn't delivered, which it wasn't, and nobody was, that I knew of.

So Alfred's holding on to the money was the best bet for now, although, of course, I didn't believe in betting, not even in buying lottery tickets, which was a controversial issue in some Christian circles. Some had the opinion that if they did win then God would have allowed it, and therefore they could give a lot of it to the church. Those same ones—usually the people barely making ends meet—said, "Just think what we could do. We could build that church building we always needed and feed the poor." And so on. Those same people seemed not to care that the lottery was a tax on the poor.

Those on the other side of the coin—although, it goes without saying I never flipped coins to make decisions—said Christians were to put their faith in God, not luck. And most of those brothers and sisters usually were doing quite nicely financially, thank you very much.

"Are you there?" Alfred said to me.

"Yes, I was just thinking."

"Well," Abner said, "we're all glad to hear that."

"No," I said. "What I mean is . . . I just had an attack of that speeding thinking that comes and goes when you fast."

"We're sick of your fast!" Mother, Abner, and Alfred yelled in unison.

That said, Mother suggested, "Perhaps, I should leave you boys alone for awhile." With that remark, she left for the kitchen. I wondered how we three had become boys all of a sudden but then let the thought drop.

"Well, this is how I see it," I said.

"Did ya hear that, Alfred?" Abner said. "This is how Detective LaFlam sees it. Well, we're all ears, so how do ya see it then?"

"Give him a break, Abner," Alfred said.

"I'm all for cutting him in half," Abner said. For what reason I didn't know because the comment seemed entirely out of context. Alfred grimaced at Abner. Then we all looked at each other. This was a challenging situation. Kingdom work wasn't easy, I knew, but there had to be an answer to what seemed to be a predicament.

"Why don't we get a hotel room," Alfred said to Abner, "until we can get a few things straightened out?"

"If ya got the money, I got the time," Abner said.

To Alfred I said, "You need to be grounded in the faith. And Abner needs support and guidance in his walk. And I'm making a commitment to see that you both make it."

"What a trooper," Abner said.

"And," I added, "we all need a solid, Bible-believing group of believers to fellowship with."

"What's that mean?" Alfred said. "All I know is I'm a new man."

"We need fellowship to grow," I said.

"Grow what?"

"Grow in the faith . . . and be witnesses . . . and give our testimonies."

"Testimonies?"

"Yeah, you have a tremendous testimony of how God healed you through my hands."

Abner said, "Ya, they like to put the newborns on the front lines."

"Uh huh, well," Alfred said, "we've got a lot to talk over." To Abner, he added, "Let's find a place to stay and then decide what we're going to do with the rest of our lives."

"Amen," Abner said.

"We can talk about the money later," I said to Alfred.

"Money? I've got lots of that. Do you mean I have to pay you for my healing? I thought—"

"No, I mean, you know, the money from my safe."

"Oh, sure, we'll talk later."

"I'll give you a ride," I offered.

"We'll say good-bye to your mother," Alfred said.

Abner and Alfred went into the kitchen, and I went out to start my Mustang. Life could be strange in the Kingdom. Here I was only a week into my fast, and not only was I about to solve the biggest case of my life; I was also about to disciple two men who were old enough to be my father.

# CHAPTER TWENTY-ONE

I got Abner and Alfred nicely situated in a downtown hotel, promising I would pick them up later to take them to the Sunday evening service at the First Church of the Manifest Presence. I left them arguing about who was responsible for the death of JFK, Abner insisting on the conspiracy theory, Alfred in favor of the lone gunman. I decided I needed to go back home and get a few things straightened out with my mother.

When I came in the door, the aroma of Norwegian meatballs struck me. It was my second favorite meal. First shepherd's pie and now this. I checked the petty thoughts in my mind and resolved to rise above them. She had a perfect right to cook whatever she wanted. I entered the kitchen, and there she was, throwing a noodle against the cupboard to see if it would stick. It did. She turned, startled.

"You're home," she said.

"We have to talk," I said.

"I know, dear. We can talk over dinner if you like."

"Sure, dinner."

Mother forked herself some noodles and topped them with the meatballs and broth; on the side she spooned some green peas. We sat at the kitchen table. As an afterthought she went to the fridge and poured me some Clamato juice.

"There, dear," she said, setting it in front of me. "And I'm sorry," she said, cutting her noodles so forcefully her plate screeched, "I should have prepared you but——"

"No need. I understand. Just because I'm not eating, there's no reason why you shouldn't have Norwegian meatballs."

"What?" she said.

"We have to talk," I said. "This is hard but, it's about the future. I think I'm going to have to move out."

"Oh, don't take it like that, dear. It's not the way it looks, really."

"No, listen, I don't care about the meatballs. I just wanted to prepare you. Most of the time I'll be itinerating anyway, and I'm pretty sure I'm going to be getting married too."

"Married? Who? Oh, she's not—"

"Who's not what?"

"Who are you going to marry?"

Mother slurped a short noodle, head bowed, her eyes looking up at me.

"I don't know who yet."

"Then . . . how?"

"There's a choice of three."

"Three?"

"Yeah, but that's not all. It looks like God has given me a healing ministry. I healed Alfred, of course. What I mean is, uh, you know, God healed him through me."

"Yes, dear, but—"

"Please, just let me finish. God has me in transition, and since the fast I'm seeing things clearer. I'm coming to a new level in my walk with God. I'll be having to leave detective work and cab driving. God has better things for me. I've got a real peace about it, and even though I don't know what it looks like yet, I'll just have to walk it out."

"Well, dear, if you have to walk it out, that's all there is to it. And don't worry, I'll manage."

She suddenly had a strange look on her face and said, "Your father will be proud."

"What do you mean, 'will be'? I'm done with that too."

"With what, dear?"

"Wanting to know who my father was. God's my Father now."

"I can understand that, dear. And I can certainly agree with your wanting to change occupations. Detective work really isn't your calling."

"Then you're all right with everything?"

"Yes, of course, dear. Whatever makes you happy is the important thing."

Changing the subject, I said, "I'm taking Abner and Alfred to church tonight. Want to come?"

"Tonight? Yes, that would be fine, dear. It would make a nice change."

"I'll pick you up later then."

"Right, dear."

I left the house not knowing where I was going. It was too early to pick up Abner and Alfred, and I wanted Mother to be left alone to digest my decision. I climbed into my car and drove in the rain. The cold, Sunday afternoon streets were splattered with the wet stuff. Where was I going? I knew my life was in transition, but how would it come out? Life was like Rummoli. Who knew how to play anymore? But play I would.

After about an hour of driving relaxation, the Golden Arches came into view. I envisioned a cool, clear drink of apple juice and pulled in. Inside the restaurant, the fries-scooping, cola-pouring, burger-flipping pawns in the American game sped on to their destiny, while I, like Wayne Gretzky, glided to the till, slowly, calmly, a confident player, skating in my own time, living in the in-between spaces.

"Large, cold apple juice," I said.

"We only have the one size, regular," she said.

"I'll have two then, please," I said.

"A number two meal?"

"No, two apple juices."

"With your meal?"

"No, just two apple juices, please."

"Here, or to go?"

"What difference . . . uh . . . here, please."

She rang my juice in, took my money, fetched my juice, put it on a tray, thanked me for my patronage, and then dismissed me with a parting sniffle. Apparently, apple juice wasn't good enough for her.

I retrieved a straw, found a table, and sat alone, feeling inferior. She might have had a different attitude if she had known I healed someone today. Fortunately—although, of course, I didn't believe in fortune—her ignorance worked in my favor. I was anonymous here. Nobody would be disturbing me, asking me to pray for them.

The Sunday evening, supper crowd milled from counter to table, lost in the narcotic aroma of grease and ketchup. Diners stuffed their heads and garbled communication. In the caged pit of colorful balls, toddlers bounced, digesting their dinners and working up a good scream to deliver to their parents when they tried to take them home. Oh, America, where the best and the worst, and those in between, devoured the spoils together.

I noticed my thinking was becoming more literate, more poetic even. No doubt fasting had loosed another gift. I sucked up the cold juice in a couple of pulls. There was nothing to do now but leave. Outside, the rain had fallen and continued to do so. I climbed aboard my Mustang and drove.

There was time to go down to the train station, so I decided it would be wise to check out the place for the Monday drop. They weren't going to roll this one by me. No, not this time. I was wise to them, real wise. Their clever, ransom drop-off location switch wasn't going to throw me. I now knew well the ways of Canute and the sisters Mulligan.

But there was something nagging at me. It was a thought that began somewhere out there, above my head, and had been trying to force its way into the top left side of my brain. And I knew enough about these things by now to know that if I did let the thought in, my conscience would start to wear on me and spoil my day.

Not that the day had started out that great. My encounter with those arrogant people at my former church, who had failed to see me truly in my spiritual splendor, had nearly discouraged me enough to forget about my spiritual sacrifice, and then my shining future in my healing ministry would have been missed, all because of them. No, I needed a more encouraging church where my gifts would be appreciated—one that would see me as I really was: a committed disciple and leader with a healing gift thrown in to boot.

But that pestering thought was trying to force its way in again. I decided to let it in and then deal with it. Why keep fighting it? Fighting it was more wearing than letting it in. Ah, so there it was. I thought that was it. Was I really supposed to be working on Sunday? That's what the thought said. So what was I supposed to do now? I was only going down to the train station to check it out. That wasn't working really. I wasn't officially delivering a ransom. I was simply out for a Sunday drive, looking for something to do while waiting for the Sunday evening service.

So what if I dropped into the train station and had a sip of water at the fountain, watched the milling masses, and maybe witnessed to a few of the lost. Sure, that was the solution. I would go and witness—that wasn't work—and if I happened to spot any suspicious kidnapper activity, well then, that would be coincidental, and I couldn't be held accountable for that. And I could just look around. That was allowed on Sunday.

But, hold on a minute. Wasn't observing the Sabbath only an Old Testament requirement? Sure, that made sense. It was a legalistic thought that had forced its way into my brain. Good spiritual thoughts wouldn't hammer away at you like that, would they—forcing their way in to annoy you? Anyway, when it came down to it, the Sabbath was really Saturday, not Sunday. So how did that work?

And then there was Paul the apostle, who said you could count all days the same? So what about healing on Sunday? The Pharisees said healing people was work, so you weren't allowed to heal people on the Sabbath. But for Christians healing was OK on Sunday, that is if your church allowed it, but then again Sunday wasn't really the Sabbath because the strict legalists wouldn't accept Sunday as the Sabbath anyway. Sunday was Sunday and the first day of the week, not the last day of the week, which was Saturday, when you were supposed to take your Sabbath rest. There, case closed.

My conscience allowed me to go down to the station and see what I could see and not feel guilty at all. That would serve those bad-conscience kinds of thoughts right, and then maybe in the future they would get convicted and not come and bother me anymore. There was no question about it; life was a continuous spiritual battle.

But what I needed now was to work on a ploy—one that would bring Canute out into the open. But how? The note said to leave the ransom in storage locker 15 and then leave the key taped under the towel dispenser in the men's washroom directly across from the main ticket counter. And then I was to leave the station immediately. They said they would be watching to see that I did. Simple enough. All I needed was a disguise. No problem there. I'd leave the key, exit the station, drive a few blocks, and then park, change, and walk back. Easy. I'd stake out the locker and, bingo, I'd collar King Canute.

So now I needed to check out the logistics of my plan. There would be no slipups this time. But what about Pen? I told her I would take her with me. A clever way to get a date but not very practical. OK, so it was a sneaky way to get a date. Either way, I'd have to tell her no; it was too dangerous. I wouldn't want to put her in harm's way. She would understand. She was the understanding kind, I could tell, having to endure the rest of her family, who were, no doubt, continually sniping at her because she was the favorite. And then plotting against her to bilk her of her inheritance. Poor kid.

But I would rescue her from all that. Joe LaFlam was her man. She would see, and then all the doubt, all the failure, all the rejection would fall from me like sandbags from a hot-air balloon. And we, Pen and I, would soar into our future together, leaving all the workaday cares of this earthbound world behind.

"Get moving . . . get moving."

The roads were clogged with Sunday drivers. But I had to forgive them. They didn't know that I was a man on a mission. How could they? So I forgave them. Yes, the future was bright. I knew that poverty would be found far from me from tomorrow forward.

I pulled up to the station, cranked a few quarters into the meter and then went in to survey my surroundings. It was a train station all right, where the smoking and chugging of the pioneering railroad, which had opened up America for business, oozed from the oaken benches and tiled floor. Busy for a Sunday too. Travellers in, travellers out. Kissing the missus, then kissing the baby; some waving good-bye, some hugging hello. People doing what they did best—simply being people.

I first checked out the ticket counter, and then, sure enough, there it was, the men's washroom right across from it. There was no chance for a slipup there. Now for the storage lockers. There they were, and there was number 15, and it was available. I decided to grab it now. Why take a chance? In with the money—I'd add that to expenses—and out with the key. Simple again. This would be a piece of cake. I had a good feeling about this. Detective work was finally going my way. A healing detective. What a combination! A gifted expert in both fields.

Yes, fasting was paying off. I was ready for them now. I was well equipped this time to overcome anything they might throw at me. But I'd need a new disguise. Canute had seen that last one. Or had he? No sense taking a chance. All I needed was a new disguise for my locker stakeout, and I was set for life.

"Psst, hey, bud," a voice said from behind a pillar. "Hey, bud," it said again.

"Who's that?" I said.

"Hey, bud."

I looked behind the pillar.

A short man, wearing a tan fedora, sunglasses, and a black trench coat said, "Hey, bud. You and Hurst are toast, you know. Nobody gets out alive."

Just when things were going good, here trouble was again.

"Things were just going good," I said. "This caper's nearly solved. Don't spoil it."

"I don't care about your caper," he said.

I moved in close to stare him down. He was about my age, and I suddenly felt compassion for him. But was it a godly compassion? He was one of my generation, who had obviously taken the wrong turn in life and was now lost in the Spelunker milieu.

"Maybe I don't have to kill you," he said. "You smell dead already."

"So, you're one of them."

"Please stand back. Further. That's better. Now here's a message for you and Alfred: We'll pick the time; we'll pick the place. Got it?"

"I think you Spelunkers need inner healing. I'm no expert in that field, but I can see you have issues. On the other hand, if you have any physical ailments, I'm the guy."

"Yeah," he said, "we heard about Alfred's heart. Just a coincidence."

I knew there was one thing all people had in common. I'd read it recently in one of those books on evangelism. If you asked to pray for them, they invariably said yes. So I popped the question.

"You need prayer for anything?"

"Huh, what do you mean? . . . Well . . . uh, yes, maybe."

"Heart?"

"No, heart's good, but I've got some arthritis in this shoulder."

"At your age?"

"Hitman-related."

"OK, fine. Let me pray for you."

"OK, bud, but don't breathe on me."

So, that evangelism theory was proven. Virtually anyone would say yes to prayer, even hitmen. After all, they were people too. I reached over and rested my hand on his right shoulder.

"Easy," he said.

I prayed a silent prayer, head bowed, and remained in that position for a minute or so, peeking a little. I saw that a few of the curious had stopped to look. And then a crowd began to gather. I was on the spot. The hitman began to fidget. He wasn't cooperating.

"It's still the same," he said.

The crowd seemed to furrow their collective brows in disapproval.

"Wait a minute."

"No, forget it," he said. "I delivered the message and now I'm leaving. Hey, hold on, what's that? Hey, I think the pain's going. What gives?"

The questioning, stunned Spelunker, testing out his shoulder joint, teetered away, suddenly oblivious to me and his surroundings. He was going before I could give him a proper witness. But there was no sense trying to catch up to him. He only wanted to kill me anyway. And he hadn't even bothered to say thanks. But that was OK because I wasn't the healer. Just something I'd have to get used to. I couldn't be expected to develop a relationship with everyone I healed. The crowd that had gathered looked at me suspiciously and then dispersed, resuming their mundane lives.

Yes, my healing ministry was intact, and tomorrow . . . but wait, who was that slipping out the far exit? Just a glimpse, but it looked like Mrs. Mulligan's right-hand man. Must have been tailing me. But that figured. No sense chasing after him either. Sure, it all figured. Yes, tomorrow was the day, and everyone agreed that work was allowed on Monday. Yes, I'd solve the case tomorrow. Success was only a day away. It didn't get any better than this. Yes, I was on a roll, and I couldn't wait to pick up my mother and my two new disciples. It was time to go to church.

Then I heard it, from a distance, the sound of the Spelunker's voice, echoing through the cavernous train station.

"No, it's still the same, you quack. But nice try."

# CHAPTER TWENTY-TWO

W e sat in the back row of the hall, the blonde Girl Guide in blue framed high on the front wall, overseeing from above the hundred or so people gathered there.

"They look like a rock band," Abner said, turning his nose up at the worship team. "Loud, too, probably." He stuck his fingers in his ears briefly for effect.

"They're charismatics," I said. "They can't help it."

"Charismatic?" Alfred said, worried. "You mean like Hitler?"

"No, not that kind of charisma," I said. "They believe that the gifts are for today."

"What gifts?"

"I'll explain later. They're starting."

"I do like the TV better," Mother said.

Associate Pastor Bernard picked up the microphone and welcomed everyone to the Sunday evening meeting of the First Church of the Manifest Presence.

Abner said, too loudly, "What kinda name is that fer a church?"

Eyes turned.

"I like it," Alfred said. "It's like Manifest Destiny."

"Hypocrites," Abner added. "All hypocrites."

"You don't know that," I whispered.

"Sure I do, they's Christians, ain't they? Just weirder ones."

Alfred whispered at Abner, "Shh, I like the feel of it here. I feel free now . . . at least until the Spelunkers find me."

Abner said, "Ya always were easy to please. No wonder ya ended up an establishment flunky."

I decided to assert my spiritual authority. "Quiet," I said.

"Power-tripper," Abner said.

Bernard finished his announcements, and the worship team took over. The congregation stood, and I followed suit—though, of course, I never gambled at cards. Alfred followed my lead, while Abner remained seated, his arms folded. Mother rested with her eyes closed. The worship team began with a lively song, which included the bold lyric, "I'll become even more undignified than this."

"Got any earplugs?" Abner said.

I realized Abner needed a great deal of inner healing, and I knew that delving into the inner workings of wounded emotions was not my ministry. Healing the body was fine, despite that last one, but he could have been lying about his shoulder. Who knew? Yes, there was no doubt I was gifted at physical healing; I had Alfred to show for it, but inner healing, I knew, was like opening a can of worms. I felt queasy. I decided I neither had the gift nor the stomach for it. I would find some inner healing experts for Abner.

But what about deliverance? What if he needed some of that too? That is, if Christians could be demonized? But that wasn't my kettle of fish either. I gagged. No, we all had to stick to our own areas of expertise. Each part doing its share. That was the secret. I needed to find someone who was gifted in both inner healing and deliverance, if in fact, theologically speaking, Christians qualified for deliverance. A bondage expert, a freedom packager, a two-in-one gifted person was needed, since the two went together—that is, if Christians could be demonized. And what about Alfred? What did he need? Who knew?

Then I realized that the whole time I had been thinking about Abner and Alfred I had also been singing. I was able to do that— think while I was worshiping. That was one thing I had been able to do since I first got saved—worship and think at the same time. I wondered if God preferred to hear me singing praises to Him or to listen to my speeding thoughts. Probably He preferred my singing; who in their right mind would have wanted to hear my thoughts? And as for our heavenly Father, who kept track of us all, He just had to have an amazing capacity to tolerate trivia.

But maybe I was being too hard on myself. After all, I was growing spiritually and now had two disciples who would benefit from that growth, and if the First Church of the Manifest Presence wasn't for me either, well, then, perhaps God was calling me to plant my own church. Preaching was probably not that tough. And any one of the Mulligan daughters had the potential to make a good pastor's wife, provided she stayed out of jail (innocent Penelope being the prime candidate, of course).

But, hold on, what was that? Or, at least, who was that, coming into the hall by the side door? Penelope? Yes, it was. Speak of the . . . . What was she doing here? She took a seat in the front row and began to worship. Maybe she was just looking for me. No, what's that? Mrs. Mulligan coming in, too, sitting by Penelope? What? No. It couldn't be. They were Baptists. Now what? There she was . . . Bertie, joining the rest of the family. Impossible. But true. And . . . and . . . none other . . . speak of the . . . there she was . . . Brittany . . . getting a lot of wear out of that peach suit. And who was that older guy with her? It was Mrs. Mulligan's bodyguard. Yes, it had to be; of course, it made sense now; who else could it be? The bodyguard had to be King Canute. A Latter-day Druid had been silently standing right there in my office, and I hadn't even known it. There they were, gathered side by side in the front row, the picture of a happy American family. But why? I sank to my seat, unable to move. My heart felt like ceasing to beat.

"No stomach fer it either, eh?" Abner said.

"Hmm . . ." I replied and gagged again.

I had to think fast. First, crimes had been committed. And the culprits were in the front row of the church. One of them was obviously a backslidden Latter-day Druid. I searched my mind for evidence. Who did I have for witnesses? The Feds? No. They had been looking for King Canute. They knew nothing about the kidnappings.

Now think . . . what had happened? Money had changed hands, that's what. But I couldn't arrest them for that. It was their money. And I wasn't the law. Hold on, what about my $20,000? They stole my inheritance. But how could I prove that? I had to think some more. There had to be an answer.

The obvious answer was that I had been had. But how had I? Lust primarily. But that was another story. Anger rose up; I choked back my empty stomach. I had to confront them. They couldn't get away with this, whatever it was. My urge to be a detective was resurfacing. How could I have so easily considered deserting my profession?

I rose, sidled out of the aisle, and strode for the front. Heads turned as I advanced on Canute and the Mulligans. A revelation came en route, and I changed my destination. The microphone. I needed to make the truth known. The worship team dialed down as I grabbed the worship leader's mike from its stand. I waved a reassuring hand at a concerned Associate Pastor Bernard.

"Listen . . . listen to me," I said confidently.

"Praise God, a prophetic word," the worship leader said, nodding.

"A Druid is here in our midst," I said. "And there he is, King Canute."

"I think we'll need to ask for discernment on that one," the worship leader said, nodding thoughtfully. "Not very edifying."

Associate Pastor Bernard left his seat and came to greet me.

"That's the senior pastor you're pointing at, LaFlam," he said.

"Your senior pastor's a Druid," I said incredulously. "No wonder the rest of us don't trust you charismatics."

"A Druid? Come on," Bernard said. "Come and sit down. You're out of order."

"I'll tell you who's out of order," I said loudly into the mike, "the whole Mulligan family." I waved my arm at all of them in the front row for effect. They stared back at me like they were embarrassed.

Bernard said softly, "Brittany's brought her family with her tonight. Don't embarrass everyone. Go sit down."

"I'm out twenty big ones, and you're telling me to go sit down. They're all a bunch of fake kidnappers."

"You've been fasting too long, LaFlam, that's your problem."

"Not so loud. I don't want to lose my reward."

Bernard nodded at two big men, who were waiting to come to his aid.

"All right," I said, "I don't want to disrupt the meeting. I know when I'm licked."

I faked going to my seat by starting off in the direction of the aisle, but then I broke sharply to my right to confront the Mulligans.

"All right, what's the score?" I demanded, eyeing each one in turn. They looked at each other as if they felt sorry for me. There was silence all around. Associate Pastor Bernard was immediately at my elbow, his usher goons behind him. I had to act fast.

"OK, where's my twenty Gs?" I said.

"That's enough," Bernard said. He motioned to the worship team to continue, but before Bernard's goons could get me, I escaped and headed quickly to my seat. I knew they wouldn't throw me out if I sat down and kept my mouth shut. They would be Christian about it.

"Nice job," Abner said, greeting me. "Ya embarrassed us in front of charismatics."

Alfred said, "What were you doing, soliciting funds?"

"Never mind, dear," Mother said, "you did your best."

The worship team started up again, no doubt to smooth over the bump in the service. I sat dazed. Worship was a blur. I had lost my inheritance and my career, such as it was, and my wives. And someone was going to pay. The only thing I had left going for me was God, and my fast, though my fast was even in question now. In hindsight, in the clear light of failure, had my fast only been works disguised as spiritual growth, and my petitions carnal? God only knew. No, I knew too.

"But try not to attack the pastor, dear," Mother said confidentially, whispering in my ear.

"Please don't talk," I said.

"Not very civil, dear . . ."

"No, my ear. It tickles my ear," I said.

"Oh, sorry, dear. You know, you might think about eating something."

The music played on. I sank into my chair. There had to be an explanation. Oh, well. I still had a healing ministry. Nobody could take that away from me. Well, God could, but He was on my side, wasn't He? I had to remain calm. There was still hope. There had to be an explanation. Yes, I had to persevere. The case was not lost. After all, I was Joe LaFlam. But why would they hire me, Joe LaFlam, to transfer their own money to themselves? Tax evasion? No, not likely; and surely not just to take my twenty grand because they continued in their game after they had bilked me of my life savings. No, there had to be another explanation, but what?

"They're fanatics," Abner said, pointing his nose at a few of the congregation dancing up front.

Alfred turned and gave Abner a look of pity and then resumed worshiping, his hands raised, getting right into it, a beatific smile on his face.

"They're only enjoying themselves," Mother said confidently.

Let my little group chat away. What difference did it make to me now? All they could do was throw us out of the meeting. That would be ironic since I was the sinless one. I had come to church with the right motive—to disciple Abner and Alfred in an atmosphere of charismatic freedom—and instead I was now having fellowship with bogus kidnappers. I definitely felt unequally yoked. But where would it all end? The trouble was I had no witnesses. Maybe Bernard. Bernard saw the first ransom note, didn't he? But he might have been in on it too. Whatever it was.

But there had to be a way. I resolved to confront them again before the service was over. Timing was everything. Reflecting on my current condition I realized that my desire for a wife had vanished, strange as that was, and as I gazed at the backs of the heads of the Mulligan daughters, I suspected that none of them was for me. Why, oh, why was all this happening? When I knew the answer to that one I would finally be able to kiss this case good-bye and get on with my life, such as it was.

And then I would dedicate my considerable healing gift to further the gospel. Yes, I would preach to the multitudes—how hard could it be? And if God found me a wife in the process, so much the better. No, I wasn't toast yet. When this was all over and my ministry begun, I might even take a few cases on the side. Sort of keep my hand in. No, the Mulligans and Canute couldn't subdue my indomitable spirit.

Joe LaFlam was many things, but he wasn't a quitter. He perhaps was incompetent in some ways, but he persevered. Yes, Joe was the salt of the earth, and he would see his life to the bitter end, which certainly wasn't now because nobody, especially him, ever died in his cases. I realized I had been thinking of myself in the third person again, a sure sign the stress of detective work was piercing my armor.

The worship team was beginning to wind down again, and Bernard moved toward the mike.

"We have some guests here tonight," he said. "Brittany's here with her family. Why don't you introduce them, Brittany?"

Brittany stood proudly, her mother and siblings smiling and turning their heads to face the congregation.

"This is my mother, Faith," she said. Mother Faith smiled some more and bowed her head humbly. Brittany continued, "And this is my older sister, Bertie." Bertie nodded to the crowd. "And this is my younger sister, Penelope . . . we call her 'Pen.'" Pen smiled and nodded too.

"And they're all criminals," I yelled from the back, unable to keep the news to myself. The bouncers again moved in my direction.

"Yer at it again," Abner said. "I don't know why I came."

"I'll give you the twenty thousand myself," Alfred said.

"You? You've got two hundred thousand of theirs you have to give back. Hey, that's right, you can give me twenty thousand and give them back a hundred and eighty thousand, and then it doesn't matter what they're up to."

"Fine."

"Thank you, Alfred," Mother said. "You always were the diplomatic one. See, dear, it will all work out."

"Yes, I believe it will," I said to myself and to Mother.

But I still needed to know. I would forever be less than a detective if I didn't follow the case to its conclusion. Money wasn't the issue now, though I couldn't believe I was now thinking that, and, upon further inspection of my thoughts and motives, I realized I was lying to myself. It was more like fifty-fifty: half the principle, half the money. That settled, I was now determined to bring this show to a close. I would confront them once more. I headed for the front and my destiny. Bernard saw me coming, as did his henchmen, and all three converged on me as I arrived at the seats of the Mulligans and Shepherd Canute.

"OK . . . enough is enough," I began to say, when the church bouncers grabbed me by the arms at Bernard's nod. A scuffle was just about to ensue when a man burst into the meeting. It was the Chicken Man in his familiar yellow jumpsuit. He ran down the aisle toward us yelling, "Stop! Stop! I tell you stop." I didn't know why he was coming to help me; perhaps he had become disgruntled with his charismatic brethren. Whatever the reason, I was glad to see him.

He collapsed in a distraught heap in front of Senior-Pastor-Druid Canute and his associate, Bernard. He was gasping, "They've gone . . . they've all gone . . . while you were in here worshiping . . . they've all gone." He began to wail. "Waaaaaaaaaaa."

The goons released me and then moved in the wailing man's direction. Since he was disturbing the meeting more than I was, this guy now took preference. The congregation, shoving chairs out of the way, was now gathering around the man, waiting for an explanation of his outburst.

"Who's gone?" Senior Shepherd Canute said.

"Everyone . . . everyone . . . except . . . except . . . us."

The crowd stirred.

Bernard said, "Who's gone where?"

"Everyone's gone, but us . . . everyone but us . . . us Christians. We're the only ones left on the planet. It's on the news . . . on the Christian news stations . . . they've gone . . . they've gone . . . away . . . all the non-Christians have been raptured."

"Raptured?" Canute said. "The lost have been raptured? By whom?"

"No one's sure," the man said, "but the whole world's at a standstill. Hollywood's a ghost town." He wailed some more.

Disbelieving, we all looked at one another.

"Hollywood? Oh, God," we all moaned.

This couldn't be happening. It was just one thing after the next. Why wasn't I allowed to finish this case? There had to be an explanation. And if all the bad people had been raptured, as the shaken chicken congregant was saying, then how was it the Mulligans were still here? Then again I knew why. We all knew. You didn't have to be good; you only had to be saved.

I caught Alfred's eye. His shoulders shrugged. No, it seemed the Spelunkers weren't behind this one. I noticed Mother had come forward and seemed more interested in Canute than in learning more about the great disappearance of the unsaved. Canute, realizing Mother was entering his space, turned from the Rapture messenger and faced her.

"Hi, Al?" she said.

"Hello, Margaret," he said.

We all looked at them, staring at each other.

"You know each other?" I said.

"Yes . . . years ago," Canute said.

"But we weren't Christians then," they said in unison to us all.

Mrs. Faith Mulligan approached the old friends, and Alfred and Abner nudged their way forward too.

"Well, the jig is up," Faith said. "He's here now, so there's no sense putting it off anymore."

"No," Canute said, "There's no sense in hiding the truth any longer."

"No, there isn't," Mother Margaret said.

"You're right," Abner said.

They looked at me, and then the whole congregation joined them in looking at me.

"What truth?" I said.

"You've caught us, dear," Mother Margaret said. "Good work."

Mother Margaret then bowed her head and said, "As you know, we haven't been entirely forthright with you."

"You haven't?" I said, confused. "What do you mean, we? I know the Mulligans haven't, but—"

"Not the Mulligans," Canute said.

"Who then?"

"Your mother and me," Canute said.

"What about everyone being raptured?" Chicken Man on the floor wanted to know, and most of the congregation suddenly wanted to know too.

"This is more important," Canute said.

"What's more important than most of the population gone?" Chicken Man said.

Feeling the need to reassure everyone, I said, "Don't worry, whatever happens, Seattle will survive."

*"This is Vancouver!"* everyone stated loudly.

To Mother Margaret and Canute and Faith, I said, "What do you mean there's something more important?"

Canute cleared his throat and then said, "Things aren't as they seem."

The people looked at each other and nodded their heads, knowingly.

"How's that?" I said, looking at my mother for an explanation. If the Mulligans weren't the problem, then I wanted to know who was.

Mother Margaret said, "We wanted to help you discover a few things, dear. Maybe that detective business isn't the best use of your time and also—"

"What?" I said. "You did all this because you think I'm in the wrong business?"

"Not me," Alfred said. "I already knew that; I was just out to kill you."

Canute said, "There's something we really have to tell you."

Canute studied the floor for a few seconds, and then he looked to Margaret and then to Faith and then to me.

"I'm your father," he said quietly.

"What? My father . . . a Druid pastor? Impossible. That would be more than even I, Joe LaFlam, could take."

I looked at Mother for support. None was coming.

"We were all hippies then," Abner said.

Alfred and Canute and Mother Margaret and Faith nodded their heads.

"Yes, we weren't Christians then," all five of them said.

A sympathetic stir issued from the congregation.

Faith Mulligan cleared her throat and said firmly, tears in her eyes, "I gave you away."

"You?" I said. "Why you?"

"Allan and I only . . ."

"Who's Allan?" I said, really confused now.

"I'm Allan," Canute said.

"Then later . . . after . . . I married someone else . . . you see," Faith said.

"You and Canute . . . and . . . and me," I said.

"Allan and I only, you know . . . and then . . . as you know, it was a different time."

"I know, you weren't Christians then."

"I didn't know," Allan Canute said.

"Neither did we," Abner and Alfred said, both staring sternly at Margaret.

"I ran away to have you," Mother Faith said, "and then I had the chance to marry Ignatius, and then my sister said she would look after the baby." She smiled kindly at Sister/Mother/Aunt Margaret. "And Iggy's family were . . . you know . . . their social status. It was best we never . . . you see . . . but I did send money, secretly, so Iggy wouldn't know . . . poor Iggy . . . his heart."

Allan said, "Your mother Faith and I have come back together after all these years, and we've finally managed to work out our church issues, and now we're planning to marry. We wanted you, John, to be part of our new family. We know there's a lot to make up for."

"But we would like to try," Mother Faith said.

I looked at Mother/Aunt Margaret. I had wondered many times how we had survived on craft-fair sales of shell necklaces and macramé.

"I'm sorry, dear," Mother/Aunt Margaret said, tears forming, "but look at it this way, you have two mothers now."

"You might have filled us in on a few more of the details," Alfred said accusingly to Margaret, and Abner nodded.

Faith said, "We're all related in a way. But, of course, we weren't in a commune or anything like that."

"No, not a commune," they all said.

"And isn't it strange how God brought us all together again," Aunt Margaret said. "And we owe it all to you, John."

"So, I'm not a John Doe; I'm a John Canute," I said.

"Sorry," Pastor/Dad Allan said.

"And you're not a Druid pastor," I said to my new/old dad.

Not-a-Druid shook his head, and then I took a good look at Brittany and Bertie and Penelope. So much for marriage. What an unlikely turn of events. I began my association with the Mulligans looking for a wife, and now I had uncovered another mother, a dad, and three half-sisters. But why had they gone to the trouble of kidnapping one another?

"But why did you go to the trouble of kidnapping one another?" I said.

"We thought it would be a way of introducing ourselves to you gradually," Mother Faith said, "in a way that you could relate to, in your line of work . . . such as it is . . . so you wouldn't be too overwhelmed all of a sudden."

I looked at Dad Canute and said, "A pastor down a manhole, collecting ransom?"

"I was under a lot of stress anyway from pastoring, and then when Faith told me about you, I kind of went over the edge . . . had a few bad flashbacks . . . you see?"

"But it was our idea!" my half-sisters proudly chorused.

"But you took my $20,000."

"We had to keep you interested," Bertie said.

"And besides," Bertie said, "I know it was wicked, but we were having fun, too, and we thought it would be a playful way to introduce ourselves."

"The family needs a lot of inner healing, dear," Aunt Margaret said.

Maybe even deliverance.

So I had been deceived. They were spoiled rich kids, extracting their pleasure from me, their half-brother, of all people. They had concocted a real life game of *Clue* at my expense. Such was the idle play of the rich. But I wasn't bitter. No, I wasn't the kind to hold onto things. I would forgive. Besides, I had to. I was one of them now.

"Yes, they truly do need healing," Bernard said. "They've been going to different churches. But now, praise God, here you all are . . . all under one roof."

As I was considering Associate Bernard's possible financial motives for his comment, the whole caper suddenly became too much. I collapsed, slowly, in stages, first to my knees and then to my face, coming to rest prone beside the now-silent Chicken Man, messenger of the Rapture of the lost.

And then I saw images on the insides of my eyelids, multitudes of people in healing lines, waiting to be prayed for. I, Joe LaFlam, a.k.a. John Canute, was being sought after by the masses. Time passed, as I prayed for thousands and thousands and then I became weary, almost about to collapse . . . when I heard a voice say . . . it was Abner's voice saying, "Too much fer 'im. How would ya like it, finding a dad and a mum and three sisters, and havin' your other mum become your aunt, not to mention healin' Alfred's heart, and then havin' all the lost raptured, and all in the same day?"

And then as an afterthought, Abner said, "Hey, I guess I'm still saved 'cause I'm still here."

"Right," Alfred said, "and I'm free too. The Spelunkers are gone."

I sat up. There they were, not the healing lines but my new relatives, and all of us Christians.

Suddenly curious, I said to Alfred, "Why were you trying to kill me?"

"Because you knew too much," he said.

"Then . . ."

"No, I didn't know about all this. I hadn't seen Margaret or the rest of them for more than thirty years."

"Me either," Abner said.

"And God brought us all together," Margaret said.

"God is good," Bernard said.

Then remembering, I said, "Why were the Feds looking for King Canute?"

"I hired them," Penelope said, giggling and proud of herself. "Actors."

"We got carried away in the novelty of the situation," Bertie said.

"Alfred's got your $200,000," I said, "minus my $20,000."

"Never mind, you have all you need now," Mother Faith said, "Dear Iggy died last year . . . his heart . . . I couldn't ever tell him about you . . . you understand, but now."

I slowly regained my feet. What was I to do? I was now a joint-heir in a rich American family, and although I was batting zero-for-three in the marriage department, with any success at all I now would not die destitute in an American big-city alley. No, I would not be an alley rat's object of scorn, buried in the refuse of ever-decaying ruin. I was a true American now.

The mystery had been solved. I was a pastor's son, and a rich one, too, with handsome half sisters—which reminded me, my fast had to end. My main petition had been denied. God obviously wasn't getting me a wife from this trio, even though I had kept up my part of the bargain. But then again, I had never been sure He had actually agreed to the deal. It was possible He had been disagreeing with my proposal all along. No, in retrospect I was positive He had been disagreeing all along. So much for my sense of being led.

And since the lost were gone—wherever—there was no reason to fast and intercede for them. All you had to know now was they were gone. Finally dealt with. Their case closed. Not that I had ever done much interceding for them in the past anyway, but I might have gotten around to it later in my fast had they not been removed from the planet prematurely. In any event the fast was ended, simple as that. I would miss the empty feeling though, and the idea that had accompanied it: I had a sacrificial purpose in life, even if only for my own benefit. But there was certainly no need to carry on down the fasting road now. God had been working out His own plan all along: Get rid of the sinners and leave the planet to us.

I looked at the Chicken Man and asked, "Has Jesus come back then?"

"No, no sign of Him."

"So," I said, "all that remains on this planet in these United States of America are Christians? And Jesus hasn't come back?"

"That's right, as far as the reporters know, we've all been left behind. And as far as I know this is Can—"

"Then God help us," I said.

"God help us," the congregation echoed.

"What's going to happen," I said, "with all the Christians let loose and no sinners to oppose us?"

"We're doomed," the congregation intoned.

"Oh, God . . . oh, God . . . I hope Jesus comes back soon," the Chicken Man wailed.

I knew suddenly I had to get outside. I ran for the rear entrance, whisking a jelly donut off the back coffee table and bursting out into the alley. Chewing lustily, I thanked God for fresh air, even though it was filled with water. Yes, the rain came down, a welcome sight. And the donut was good. I hoped it wouldn't tie my colon in a knot.

A cat, which my exit had disturbed, ran under a dumpster, seeking an escape from me and the rain. I noticed, thankfully, that the planet felt lighter, and that the alley no longer seemed depressing, seen as it was now through the dilettante eyes of a nouveau riche. Indeed, with the lost really lost now, we were all rich.

But what were we to do? What were we to do now that the potential for evil had been removed from the planet with the unexpected departure of all the sinners? One thing was for sure, my work had ended. There would be no need for detectives anymore. My kind had seen their day. Really, how bad could things get now with only us Christians here to subdue the planet? No, the days of murder and mayhem had ended once and for all. My job was done.

I heard the Guide Hall door creak open, and I turned to see Bernard coming toward me.

"Of course, you know," Bernard said, standing beside me and looking up at the falling rain, "Sidney's been known to get a little hysterical about the Rapture."

"Sidney?"

"In the yellow jumpsuit. He gets mixed up and imagines things from time to time. Harmless really."

"Oh . . . I see, yes, of course. Sure, that figures . . . of course, I knew it all along. I knew things couldn't be that easy."

So, the lost were still with us. I had been a victim of wishful thinking, though, of course, I never made wishes, except when I blew out my candles on my birthday cake, but everyone knew that those kinds of wishes were only pretend. No matter, I was rich, and now there was no need to give up my life's calling.

I, Joe LaFlam, could easily blend my detective work and my healing ministry. And now I wouldn't have to rely on income from my cases. And now, of course, cab driving was history. And now I would have a bigger office in a better building in the heart of the city. No, my new family meant well, trying to rescue me from my chosen profession, but I needed to maintain my true identity. I was a detective first and proud of it. God would understand too. A life of fasting and self-denial wasn't for me. I just wasn't the kind to itinerate.

I said, "We should break the news gently to Alfred."

"Alfred?"

"Yeah, the Spelunkers are still with us. But, no matter. The main thing is that the kidnapping case has been solved, and the Christians weren't really criminals; they were simply Christians trying to get along in this world, Christians doing the best they could with the pasts they were dealt—though, of course, I don't gamble at cards. And I, Joe LaFlam, well I . . . will always be me."

"I see," Bernard said. "Well, that sums things up quite nicely. But I think there's one other thing you should know."

"What's that?"

"It's about your new sisters. Brittany told me earlier tonight that they were all adopted."

"They were? Wow! Oh, wow! But, hold on. Hmm, how does that work?"

"You might want to take a real close look at Deuteronomy," Bernard said.

"Ah, God's really got a sense of humor, hasn't He?"

"Yes," Bernard said, "and He certainly does work in mysterious ways."

From the hall came the sound of worship. "I'll become even more undignified than this" swirled out into the dank night, paused, and then flew on its way, inevitably upward. Satisfied, I licked the sugar from my lips, gazing up at the dark sky's falling drops.

"No kidding, eh?" I said.


The End